.

c

o

p

e

For more information, find CCM at:
http://copingmechanisms.net

The Prodigal

a novel by

Alexander J. Allison

I

♠ ♥ ♣ ♦

Sometimes, Martin forgets his age. Rather, he can't immediately remember it. When asked, there's this definite, horrible pause between question and answer. It is a pause charged enough to mean anything. Martin is twenty-one – an age not worth lying about.

Each day, he will wake naturally, proceed to masturbate over online pornography, then browse the BBC website for up to an hour. News should only be experienced in the wake of an orgasm. Days are marked and passed by this ritual. Masturbation is Martin's debauched form of calendar.

Martin is twenty-one and cannot grow a beard. He likes to imagine awards for himself.

BBC Online's Person of the Year

Best Martin Award

Martin is on Gmail chat with David. They are planning how they will *take down* Full Tilt Poker.

"We need an inside man," David says. "He needs to *fuck* the innards of their corporate bowels and he needs to put his dick so far up their comfort zone that they bleed internally."

"Okay. Yeah," Martin says.

"Sorry, that was very serious and threatening. I don't think I'm an angry person. You know I'm not."

"I know you're not an angry person," Martin says.

"What are you doing?"

"There is a bit of fluff caught under my space bar. I'm trying to get it out, it's annoying me."

At twenty-one, everything seems far too legal. Every possibility is far too plausible. People have begun to ask what Martin does, rather than questioning what it is that he wants to be. Martin has a 2:1 degree and not much else. He could start work tomorrow, if he wanted to. He doesn't. For now, he tells people that he is a professional online poker player. For now, Martin feels just about willing to continue existing.

Martin is thinking of the word 'generational' and smiling.

Generational

"Becky invited us to a home game on Friday," David says.

"Okay, that could be good. Good good good. I think I might enjoy that. I might enjoy that a lot. Good. Goody goody good good. Could you pick me up if we go?"

"Yeah. I think so."

After university, Martin moved back into his parents' home. This went unquestioned. This had been assumed. It had not merited a formal discussion. Martin's room is awesome. It is kitted out with:

- an independent landline
- a 40" flat screen television complete with every current games console and a vast selection of (mostly unplayed, still packaged) games
- a large lava lamp
- a wine rack
- a limited print series of Paolozzi artworks
- two large, crap laden book cases
- a mini-fridge

Martin's cleaner is due to make her daily round in five minutes. Her name is Elza. Elza is professionally qualified to remove layers of dead skin from surfaces and objects.

"We should totally start our own casino," David says.

"Okay, yeah. That sounds good. That sounds like a project I could commit to. A casino would be a good addition to my brand. Where should we open it?"

Under Martin's desk, the cream carpet is blotched with a scab of dried red wine that he likes to toe at. It is a distinctively middle class stain; it is a secret that only he and Elza share.

"London, obviously. Wait, maybe no. Hmm. It just occurred to me: say we have a working budget of a million pounds. To get things up and running will drain our whole budget, then we wouldn't have any kind of float."

"I just said "One Million" in an evil-villain voice. Why do we need a float? I don't think we should open it here, by the way. If we do this, I want to get away."

One Million

Get away

"Say someone comes in on the first day and bets £500k on Red and wins. We lose our whole float and have to close down. I haven't thought this through yet. It has started to seem really hard."

"Hang on, my mother is calling me. Brb."

"Okay. You have made me very aware of the fluff on my keyboard. It's mostly just crumbs. I always eat here."

"Me too. I was just thinking: I don't know what like five or six of the buttons on my keyboard do. I am going to experiment after. This will be fun."

Martin's mother looks like she used to be beautiful. She is wearing a t-shirt and tracksuit bottoms. No bra is necessary. Sometimes, she'll refer to this look as her 'Cozy Day Look'. Cozy days are increasingly common. As his mother speaks, Martin imagines her in a 'Murdering Day Look.'

Axe and gun and gun and axe

"Elza is coming now, Martin," she half-shouts from his doorway. In profile, she looks sleepy and agitated.

"Are you okay?" Martin asks.

"Did you eat your breakfast?"

Martin holds up an empty plate by way of response, turning back to his screen.

His room tends to get messy very quickly. The epicentre of mess trends towards the computer. Martin considers that an archaeologist investigating his room would note it as a '*site of particular interest*'.

Arty fact

"*Your father and I need to speak about your finances, Martin,*" she shouts, leaving without having entered.

"Okay, cool," Martin replies blandly, deafly.

"I can't be bothered finding out what they do any more. The buttons I mean. Do you think, at some point, there will be a museum of, like, old technology?"

"I think there is one, maybe. I don't know. Try Googling it," David says.

"Okay."

Martin knows that he will not Google whether there is already a museum of old technology. He briefly ponders whether a computer would prefer to be in a landfill or a museum.

Updating

Gmail indicates that David has been typing for a while. Soon, a long block of text appears. Blocks of text seem imposing to Martin.

"You know those people who are always asking about music and say they're really into music? I don't get that, man. I can't relate to that. They completely dedicate themselves to keeping on top of other people's creativity. It's like they're using other people's creativity to express their own individuality. It's bullshit man. Music isn't an activity, like how watching a film is. I never *just* listen to music, it's always music and something else."

"Seems dumb when people accuse musicians of 'selling out.' Selling out is underrated. I would sell myself out every day. We are all hypocrites," Martin says.

iTunes has frozen. It does this every few hours. In these moments, Martin feels highly self-aware. Silence becomes suspicious and inappropriate. Silence feels like a threat. Silence feels like choking. Silence might mean thought.

"Do you think internal bleeding would hurt? It must be really warm. I reckon it feels like swallowing a big gulp of tea after having eaten a lot of ice cream."

"I think bruises are sort of like internal bleeding," Martin says. "I get random bruises on my legs quite often."

"Must be a gay thing, hahahah," David says.

"Fuck off, David."

Elza has entered the room and begun vacuuming. No mutual acknowledgement of another human presence is passed between Martin and his maid. Ritual dictates that Martin is to remain at his desk or on his bed until the cleaning process is complete. Elza's movements are slow and thorough. She appears very occupied by her work, staring deep into the carpet. Elza has spent much time in this space. She knows the texture of Martin's smells: the stresses and lulls in each of his odours. She knows the ripeness of his sweat, the coarseness of his shame. Perhaps she can even trace each of his lies, each of his failings. Redoubling over the entranceway, Elza brings forgiveness, brings renewal. At the wine stain, she pauses. This spot, this scar, this permanence: it has become her greatest shame, the mark of her mortality. Martin considers that really, this is Elza's room.

"The vacuum would seem dangerous and exciting to my archaeologist," he thinks.

2007

♠ ♥ ♣ ♦

It is Martin's final parents' evening. The school treats these evenings as a chance to cram tea and sandwiches in the questioning mouths of trustees. All interviews and meetings take place in the newer wings of the school. Here, there are no leaks; the paint is not peeling. Here, there is a palpable smell of detergent.

Martin's father is not present. He has not been able to attend on account of some significant event that Martin had failed to listen to the details of. Martin feels no resentment about his father's absence; he thinks practically, noting that it will speed up the time taken to humour each of his teachers.

Martin's mother is pale. Closing in on fifty, she is yet to learn how to apply make-up with any degree of confidence. Wisps of fine hair hang around her jawline, creating a trippy effect where natural light catches her face more often than it ought to. Despite their living together, Martin has not been around his mother for an extended period in weeks. Now, they sit clerically beside each other without passing any acknowledgment of the other's presence.

Google has previously informed Martin that the hairs are called *lanugo* and are a symptom of *anorexia nervosa*. He has since forgotten this.

Pity

Martin feels highly aware that in the absence of his father, his teachers are failing to display the levels of enthusiasm that he is accustomed to. Since Martin's father is a major trustee, he is de facto a major pupil. For years, Martin has been 'full of potential'. His school is very expensive and each teacher has their own office. Teachers are referred to as 'tutors' and offices are not to be used for sexual affairs. It seems to Martin that there is little point to an office that is not being used for sexual affairs.

Martin doubts that his mother will relay his teacher's reports back to her husband. He feels unsure that she will remember having been here. She is merely going through the motions of parental servitude, playing the game of responsibility, pretending that she knows what she is doing - just like everyone else.

Guise

Earlier today, Charlie Crabtree issued a hollow threat that given the slightest opportunity, he would fuck Martin's mother in an instant. At numerous points through this evening, Martin has taken measures to parade his mother in Charlie's line of sight, making discreet, provocative gestures signalling his acceptance of their inevitable union. Thus far, Charlie has been making an unconvincing effort at pretending not to notice.

Charlie's father looks like the villain from a bad movie.

One million dollars

"Martin," his mother snaps. They have reached the front of the queue for Mrs. Holmes, English tutor. Mrs. Holmes smells of tobacco. Her breasts are small and her teeth are yellow. She is human too, Martin reminds himself.

While Mrs. Holmes speaks in the direction of Martin's mother, Martin occupies himself with the lighter in his pocket. He thinks about its weight. He thinks about its smoothness. Martin can feel it pressed into his skin, mocking his own desperation. The lighter is a symbol, the lighter is the outdoors, resistance, freedom.

Fraternité

Mrs. Holmes appears to have just used the cliché "addictive personality" in reference to Martin. The term seems vague. Does this mean people are drawn to him? Could it mean he's infectious?

"Fuck off," Martin thinks. "Fuck right off you old bag."

He is now visualising how he would like to kick Mrs. Holmes, whilst fingering the flame switch of his lighter.

Pyromaniac

Martin is not an angry person. Like every teenager, he is misunderstood. Martin knows what's best. He knows everything.

II

♠ ♥ ♣ ♦

Martin knows nothing. His continued existence is accountable to a combination of incredible luck and not yet fucking up in an unforgivably bad way.

On record, he has attempted suicide twice.

The first incident came shortly after the move, before Martin had been diagnosed with any kind of depression, before that word had become part of their lives.

[Fluoxetine Hydrochloride – x two 20mg capsules, to be taken once a day at a regular time]

It had been their family home for sixteen years. It had been a part of the family for longer still. Even after they gutted it, it had still looked like a home.

The new house was hollow. It was a building: material and earth and dirt. Martin's room had been assigned. He can recall having been overwhelmed by the space. On first entering the room, he felt naked. More than that: stripped. Made bare. It was a real space, devoid of the technologies that dictated the rituals of his existence. This space was raw and awful. The only thing close to a screen was his window: a single, large and heavy pane that insisted on filling the room with the day. This was a space to be filled with life, their lives, real lives. Lives made up of relationships based on objects, made of possessions and formed in memories. This space created a

grand

, complex *pressure*, which only Martin had

seemed aware of.

It ran
under
the surface of his skin;
a viscous-stream,
bubbling feverishly
through
every moment
he
spent
indoors.

It wasn't like little pieces of past owners were comfortingly caught between the floorboards and behind the tiling. There were no stories in these walls. No happy dreams or empty hopes. This space was haunted by *want*: by the desire to be filled up to its edges with life. His life. From now, this would be the life he was to inherit. This was Martin's legacy. This house was to become the designated centre of Martin's universe and his reality's primary reference point. This was all he had to live for, and this was simply not enough.

It was unclear what Martin's father had hoped to achieve by their move. It wasn't as though they had previously been confined by a deficiency of space. They hadn't even moved that far. If it was space that they had really desired, why not leave London entirely? Worse still, they had been arrogant enough to retain ownership of the old house, for reasons described to Martin as 'just in case'. This seemed like some ineffable form of torture, an unfair, undue punishment on his real, beloved home.

In the weeks following their move, Martin's father's hands began shaking, fist forming and tensing. His hands shook. His father's hands shook.

Martin felt a profound guilt about betraying his first home. It was as though he was wiping out his past, turning reality into memories, memories that could only fade. Martin felt that he was depriving the house of himself, and felt even worse about taking up yet more space in an already overcrowded city.

All this fear, this aversion: it was more than horror. It felt biological, inoperable. These were not the ghosts of a previous, unrequited pain. This fear could not be extracted and dissected through therapy. This fear of space was a discriminate reaction, akin to how the body responds to the snake, the spider, the parasite. This space conjured an illness beyond all reason.

Outside the internet's vast planes, reality is so trite, so pale. Senses are lazy, or something. Real space is bound by limit and Martin is a no limit solider for life. Physical reality is the internet's brutish sibling.

In the week leading up to the first incident, Martin thought compulsively about bookshelves. He thought about their weight, their presence and their power. Martin thought about how much space J. K. Rowling occupies in the world. His hands had seemingly inherited his father's new tendency for spontaneous bouts of

ji

tter

ing.

Impaired dexterity proved an impractical trait for a teenager with suicidal tendencies. It was an issue to be worked around.

By the tipping point, Martin had not left his new home in over two weeks. When he did, it was over the second floor terrace. He returned with a broken femur, three cracked ribs, a fractured ankle, a dislocated shoulder, two shattered collarbones and severe internal and external bruising. One doctor had described it as 'impressive'.

It would be another three weeks before Martin was next permitted to leave.

"Never again," he had promised his mother.

III

No one can pay for a smoker's privilege at the Lyceum Casino. Martin has been playing for an hour, and the twangs of withdrawal are beginning to pinch. Since 2007, smokers have been forced outside. Now, to be a smoker is to be an outsider. Martin's entire smoking career has been spent in fresh air. Even here, in the romance of the poker room, there is no toxin-laden haze. Here, there is just the smell of men. Looking down to 8♣6♦, Martin squelches against the remains of some thoroughly pulped nicotine gum and folds with a grimace. Poker is a game of patience. Or not, whatever. Martin imagines that the churning of his jaw makes him look ferocious, like a pissed off dog.

Masticate

♠ ♥ ♣ ♦

Outside, the morning chill makes everyone appear to be a smoker. As tourists stream past the Lyceum, clouds of steam boil from their lungs. The air sweats a rich smell of tarmac.

"I feel very rich and powerful," Martin thinks, returning into the warm.

In London, you're never short of a game. Take your pick from £1/£1 to £10/£20. There's a seat with your name on it. Every casino in the West End runs a poker room. Of course, all the real money is in the pits. Once dusk hits, the grinders stream out to the illegal games and the drunks hold court.

Martin sits back down, waiting to be dealt in. His stack sits as he left it. In this space, reputation counts for more than petty theft. He strokes one shoe across the plush carpet, whilst winding the toe of the other purposefully into the floor. He semi-consciously riffles two stacks of chips as the action is passed around. He is demure: sure of himself, in his natural environment.

Yeah, bitches. I'm back

In Martin's periphery vision, a girl is scanning every shoulder in the room. Her uniform is black and tight. Their uniforms are always black and tight. The poker hall offers semi-professional massages, without (to Martin's awareness) prompting much interest. It is a windowless room. The air is dark and full. The exclusion of natural light is a casino technique, used to prevent patrons from keeping track of time. You won't find a clock in the casino. Dust motes swirl notably under certain areas of the lighting and before the 24-hour sports channels. You won't find a mirror on the casino floor. Mirrors destroy illusion. A mirror shows you, with all your spots and that mop of greasy hair. A mirror reveals the real you: the loser, the degenerate.

In seat three, a middle aged black man has shoved for £260 to steal an average sized pot. He slides the dealer a pound chip and smiles. The dealer returns his grace and raps the donation on the iron tip box.

I feel good, because I am a ferocious dog and I will get you if you pull that shit on me

Martin is happy to seem happy. His table is full of casino regulars. Martin is the youngest human in the room by a notable and observable gap.

♠ ♥ ♣ ♦

In 2003, an accountant and amateur player called Chris Moneymaker won the World Series of Poker Main Event. Within three years the Main Event field had grown by 1000%. Poker had exploded. Internet poker sites were creating self-made . teenage millionaires. The game got tough. A new class of young, educated white men came to dominate Hold 'Em, using online forums to exchange advanced theory and hand histories. Here in the Lyceum, there is no evidence of this change. The field is still soft. Money flows freely. It is still 2002.

Here, the play moves deceptively. Rhythms change, shifting round diets and tempers. One orbit takes ten minutes. A hand later, one decision might take the same. The game circles like a bird, the pot acting as its gravity. At the moment of a fold, the ritual quickens, reborn.

An elderly Asian man approaches the table from the cash desk. His tiny, tan hands struggle to manage two small stacks of loose, high denomination chips. Asking for a rack would be below him. With a look of vague consternation, the man settles down at the opposite end of the table. His face is streaked with fine creases. Martin hates playing against old people. They act slowly and tend to add nothing to the action. Now settled, the old man begins to count his chips. His face has tightened up, giving him an expression that appears to be a mixture of seriousness and drowsiness.

Martin imagines that he should be feeling some sense of endearment towards the old man, to the elderly in general. Instead he is spiced with a desire to stroke the man's face. It seems too easy to feel disgusted by old people. The man's head looks like a depressed balloon.

Hans Moleman

The Lyceum is notably understaffed today. On a table to the right, the dealer looks over his shoulder, publically gesturing that it is time for his break. It is evident that dealers don't care about the fortunes of the players, the scum at their table. They earn the equivalent of three big blinds an hour.

The hall's best-tipped waitress *(buxom/bleached/mid-twenties)* leans forward over the middle-aged black man at the opposite end of the table, knowingly flashing Martin a bit of tit as she does so.

"She is doing that for me," he thinks. The man probably stinks of an eight-hour poker session. It is a smell somewhere between fine cheese and cheap meat. The waitress winks. She was made for winking.

Martin sits on his hands, alternately raising himself left to right in time with an absent tune. Internally, he begins to swear loudly. Brilliant streams of ***fuckshittingcuntballs*** flow in every mental direction.

Do not fear losing. Do not honour your chips -

> *Confucius – World Series of Poker Main Event Champion, 5th Century BC*

To the left is a man who probably drinks straight from the carton and cuts his toenails in the living room. He speaks a little too loudly, as though he were slightly deaf or much further away. Martin decides that meditation should sound like a sat-nav.

"Check," the man says.

In this state of heightened concentration, Martin feels important and business-like. It is a noiseless zone. The yogic tone has developed into a karate chant. Karate seems far cooler than meditation.

Haiiiiii-ya

Martin is roaming in what his mother had once called a 'cognitive dead-space'. He is working his plaintive expression deep into the consciousness of each man around the table.

I am here and I am here to win

I am here and I am here to win

I am here and I fear the bin

I am beer and I smear the grin

Over the next two hours, Martin loses all of his chips. He does not feel too strongly affected by this.

Outside, it has warmed up considerably. Couples move about busily, communicating through gloved and hooded gestures. When Martin leaves Leicester Square, a sports car speeds past him.

"*Vroom!*" Martin thinks.

Martin is in a gym. He is surrounded by a labyrinth of pulleys and handles. With the bold posture of an executioner, Martin forces his bicep into wailing out a hundred lifts. Annual membership is priced at £495 (excl. VAT). Martin's mouth is thick with spit. He is light headed, 5'8 and 129 lb.

In school, Martin had enjoyed distance running. Distance running had seemed like the white rice of athletics: bland, monotone, a staple. Nothing exceptional is expected of a distance runner. Words like 'endurance', 'persistence' and 'consistency' carry an attractively hollow tone. Though they are of no inherent virtue, there is an assumed value to their spirit. Endurance, persistence and consistency: qualities that can be neatly mapped to the building of character; about as clean as words can be.

In Martin, the triumvirate spirits of endurance, persistency and consistency are melted down to a sheer cliff of stubbornness. Ignoring the harsh, sharp pains that are cutting through his elbow and forearm, he lifts and lifts and lifts and lifts, lifting a year's exercise into this afternoon. Martin lifts away his frame and the backlog of never-ever-used annual memberships. He lifts and lifts and lifts in competition with imagined ghost-runs, the computer set high-score.

Eighty-two/Ate-ee-three/Eight-four

Around Martin, men are being men. They wear shorts. Towels hang around their necks. When they stand, their backs are straight.

One hundred/one-one-one/hundred-two

Martin's hand is dripping. He feels dizzy. He is biting at the air. The weight falls from his fingers. Heads turn.

"You okay?" someone asks.

"Yeah, yeah. Feeling good." Martin's arm hangs by his side: the dead remnants of a limb. His eyes are flush with water. His forehead throbs. "That's me though. That's me done now. I'm done for today."

Soon, there will be McDonalds. Soon, there will be sleep.

IV

♠ ♥ ♣ ♦

It is 10pm. Martin is at Becky's house, where he has been playing poker with David, Becky and her boyfriend, Craig, for the last three hours. The four are playing a 'friendly', 10p/20p cash game. The action is excellent. Almost every hand goes to the flop. David has rebought twice. There is around £150 on the table. Martin has chipped up slightly and is now playing a stack of around one hundred and fifty big blinds. Martin and David are sat next to each other on one side of a high, square table.

"Is anyone else really uncomfortable?" Martin says. "Your chairs are shit, Becky. Buy some comfortable chairs." Martin squirms, lithe in his chair.

"That pain is caused by a build up of Lactic Acid," David says. "You need to exercise more, Martin."

"Yeah, Martin. You're one big Lactic Sack," Becky says.

Slacktic

"If you don't start working out, you're going to atrophy into a Golemy little gimp."

"I'm okay with that," Martin says, riffling a stack of twenty chips.

"Guys. Hey, guys," Craig says, "Guys, look at this. Look. The milk that we buy fits perfectly on the shelf of our fridge. I really like that. Do you see? It makes the milk seem so much more satisfying. I keep buying us this specific milk, because I feel like it has been designed that way, just for our fridge." Craig stresses each '*our*'. Martin knows that Craig has only recently moved into Becky's home.

"Stop talking shit and finish the tea, Craig," Becky says. Craig turns away, smiling a wide, smug beam. He looks like a Joker card.

Martin only knows Craig in the context of these home games, having played with him four times previously. Craig is loose-passive, the worst kind of poker player.

David is rambling. "I really resent the old couples on those property shows who are like, 'Oh, but we *need* four bedrooms in case everyone we know stays over at once.' Or, 'Oh, but we *couldn't* settle for four acres, we need six!' Wankers." David throws in his big blind to punctuate his anger.

"I hate seeing people on Antiques Roadshow jizzing themselves at the value of their old shitty vase, then feeling the need to make out like it's invaluable to them," Craig says. "'Oh, I could never sell it. It is priceless to me.'" Craig places his hands on his cheeks in a *Home Alone* pose to say this.

"Why are you watching Antiques Roadshow?" Becky says.

"My mum likes it, fuck off."

"Hold on – Craig, are you wearing a watch?" David says. "Who the fuck wears a watch?"

"What is this? I'm not here to be picked on, are we playing or what?" Craig smiles, creating a pretence of unaffected calm. He slides his hoodie sleeve down over his watch.

"Tell your woman to play then," David says, clucking his tongue impatiently.

"Oh shit, is it on me? I didn't even know," Becky says, folding.

On arrival, Martin and David had found Becky and Craig watching a video on YouTube. Craig insisted on reloading the video from the beginning. Becky had rolled her eyes and moved off to set up the chip stacks. The video was a comedy sketch by Peter Kay. Craig had insisted the video was funny, that it was about to get funny, that a great bit was coming up. He had laughed loudly and harshly throughout the video. After, he had noted that they were close to being the millionth viewer.

Martin is thinking about how Becky manages to give out an impression of sexual confidence and maturity, despite remaining very plain looking and flat chested. Becky is the kind of person who would insist on making sure that a circle was the right way round. If Martin squints, Becky looks a little like Peter Kay. She speaks in a harsh, nasal manner, as though her words are being forced through an invisible, choking stranglehold, or some perpetual cold. Martin is dubious of the illusion that this might imbue her words with value. Becky is a spewtard player – hyper aggressive.

"You know how reincarnations work, right?" David says.

"Raise," Becky says, moving £1.50 into the pot. David cuts out a call and continues.

"Well, your level of being in the next life is supposed to be determined by how you behave in this life, right? Well, how do you account for population growth? Does it mean that suddenly, more chimps and dolphins and dogs and whales and other higher mammals are somehow living more moral lives?"

The flop comes J♦4♦8♦. David checks quickly and Becky begins to carve out a bet.

"Also, what about the stagnation of social mobility? Does that indicate that somehow our moral capacity has peaked? Did it plateau somewhere around the time that human rights were invented?" David insta-mucks to Becky's pot sized bet.

"Death seems fucked," Martin says distractedly, washing and riffling the deck.

"Dude – we nearly died on the way here," David says. At the top of Martin's road, an SUV had almost turned into David's car.

"Yeah, that was good. It felt really real." Martin repeats the words 'really real' in his head a few times, like a baseline. Neither Becky nor Craig are showing any signs of being engaged by this morbid anecdote.

Dull fuckers

"Can I pick the next song?" David asks, "Becky, your taste in music is terrible."

"Maybe some people don't have taste," Martin says, dragging in a pot.

"Everyone has taste, Martin," Craig says, "Everyone wants to believe that they have an artist's eye. It's basic conceit. It's evidenced everywhere. For example: at some point in your life, you must have asked a stranger to take your photo. That stranger will always try their best for you. The stranger will take a lot of pride in the image. Most will even take a second shot, just in case. Or what about the way poor people curate their bedrooms? You've got to admit that shows some kind of taste."

"Maybe. Seems like no one has a sense of what is beautiful though. They know what is ugly, but they don't know what is beautiful."

"If you want to really provoke someone," David says, "Tell them that their child is ugly. Tell them: 'that's a fucking ugly child you've got there.'"

"Thinking about this makes me feel so fucked," Martin says. "It's like when we were chatting about music last week. I said to David that if I had ever wanted to get like, really into music, and obsess about trivia and get a band's logo tattooed on my arm, that moment has so passed now. I will never have that. That can never be who I am."

"You know what makes me feel most fucked?" David asks, "When I've just watched a sex scene in an old film, like one from the 70s or 80s, and then you look up the actress in the film on imdb, and of course, she's really old now, but you still want to do the younger version of her? That's what makes me feel most fucked up."

"You're sick," Becky says, dealing.

"What you going to do about it?"

"I'm going to take all your chips."

"This is war," David says.

"Poker is always war."

"No, war is war," Martin says. He looks down at J♣2♣ and mucks.

"Are we at war at the moment?" Craig asks.

"Poker is war," Becky reminds him.

"I think we're at war," David says. "I don't get the guys who keep insisting we should 'support our troops', like they're on a football team. Like we have a choice of which side we're on. They make out like the people are really brave to be out there. That just seems dumb to me. Don't they have like tanks and machine guns? Aren't they fighting against like peasants?"

"You're thinking of Vietnam," Becky says, "Anyway, I don't really care about the war. Is it awful to say that? I just don't care. I'm not angry at the troops though. It seems like it isn't their fault."

"What the fuck are you guys talking about?" Craig says. "Are you seriously saying you don't support British soldiers?" Craig goes to stand up, but seems to change his mind. He hovers above his chair for around five seconds before sitting back down.

"Don't speak like that to me," Becky says, turning to him. "I never said that I didn't support them." David makes the sound of a whip.

WHOO-PA

"No, it is fucked to say that. You two need to grow up," Craig says, gesturing with his mug at Becky and David.

"We should go to war with Full Tilt Poker," Martin says. "We should hold Tom Dwan hostage."

"That would be the most boring hostage tape ever."

"He could be our inside man, David. Dwan could develop Stockholm syndrome. We could brainwash him or something. Then he could go back and fuck their corporate bowels."

Dwan-holm syndrome

"Being a hostage would be pretty surreal. It seems like something everyone should experience," Craig says.

"Becky's got your cock hostage," Martin says. David throws him a fist bump.

"Being a hostage would be really humbling. It would make me feel really human. I feel most human when I Google an obscure question and see that someone else has already asked it in Yahoo Questions," David says.

"Did you know that Google is accepted as a word in Microsoft Word?" Craig says.

"Shut up, Craig," Becky says.

Somehow, Martin and Becky have built a huge pot. The board reads 9♠9♣T♠A♦.The pot is worth around two hundred big blinds.

"All in," Becky says. Martin reluctantly slides his Q♠J♠ into the muck, grimacing. Becky flips over 7♣7♠ and stands up, fist pumping.

"MOVE BITCH, GET OUT THE WAY, GET OUT THE WAY BITCH, GET OUT THE WAY!"

"You had me beat," Martin says, "I folded the open-ended straight-flush draw." David and Craig look across the table at each other, then back to Martin.

"You didn't actually," David says, astonished.

"I did," Martin says, scrambling around in the muck for his proof. "Look, see."

"That's terribad, dude," Craig says.

"Whatever," Martin says. His tea is cold. Becky stacks her chips, beaming. "I'm going to add on," Martin says, laying £20 on the table.

"You can buy it out my stack," Becky says, needling him.

Martin is unaware of having played any poker in the last half hour.

He is losing the war.

It must be his turn to lose.

Disciplined Poker vs. Martin's Poker

♠ ♥ ♣ ♦

Knowing when to walk away from the table	Walking in a circle back to the table
Waiting for a better spot	Hoping they're on a missed draw
Avoiding the pros	LOL, I'm so pro
Playing the man, not the cards	Playing with shoelaces
Conceding defeat gracefully	Humming 'We are the Champions' – Queen, 1977
Sticking to a bankroll	Too balla for a bankroll
Tipping the dealer	Cursing the dealer
Staying alert	She's flashing a bit of tit again
Sticking to tea	Another Budweiser, please

V

Martin stands in the midst of a large, coated crowd. King's Cross is no place to stand still. This is a place of movement. There are arrows on the floor that insist on flow, on pace. People bob from toe to heel. They are a swaying, bodily mass in communal vigil. Their wait will climax when the last of them concedes, slipping the loaded backpack off of his worn shoulders. For now, smokers lurk near doorways, huddle-bound by complaint-based-camaraderie. Their mutterings are few and clear.

Hurry.   Late.   Ridiculous.   Again.

Only tourists seem intimidated by bomb scares. This will be their premium anecdote, Martin considers. This is their life on the line. A bomb scare is infinitely more engaging than the routine case of a potential car crash.

Martin imagines Kings Cross lying empty, virginal beneath the streets. The stillness of the image is unnerving. Martin knows that he would not want to be the first to re-submerge.

The winter seems present and severe. Impatience thumps like held breath. They all know that it will be half an hour before the doors reopen. Five minutes have passed. Those who are just arriving, joining the back of the fleshy mass: they have no idea of the pain that the others have gone through.

This morning, the ***job*** word came up again. Martin had been asked and was forced to provide the *only correct answer*. ***Job*** is a dirty, messy word. It does not look English. ***Job*** means hands, means schedules and gossip, means bright eyes and sore souls. ***Job*** means alarms and assessment and family friendly smoking area kiosk lighting managerial staff overtime Christmas parties.

Sometimes, Facebook speaks of jobs, speaks of those taken in by the word. Martin hears little and cares less about the occupations of those who stepped straight out of university into a corporate reality. To Martin, they are the weak. The unbrilliant. Yet they are the ones claiming all the best prepositions: the ons, the ups, the forwards and the withs.

Rumours stream from the front of the pack. Talk of fires. Talk of a fatality. Now, a faceless cry of *MOVE BACK, P-LEASE*. The shuffling begins.

♠ ♥ ♣ ♦

Stepping out of Leicester Square station, Martin lights the cigarette he has been toying with since Russell Square. It is important to look and feel cool on entrance into a casino. It's a personal jackpot for Martin each time that he avoids being asked for ID. Across the street, road works are splitting a stream of commuters. A goggled and fleeced man is drilling with a serious facial expression. The man seems unfazed by the abounding stress that he appears to be generating. Some block their ears as they pass, throwing the man a haughty grimace. Waves of noise bounce off the traffic. As he walks, Martin concentrates on being able to hear the drill for as far as possible. By the time Martin reaches The Lyceum, he can't be sure if the noise is real, or just hanging in his ears.

News of potential bomb scares will not yet have reached the casino floor. The poker room is a space cut off from reality, where money dictates the flow of all relations. There is an air of mischief to the room. People speak out the corners of their mouths. Things seem on the cusp of legal behaviour.

This microcosm has its own language. It's a living lexicon. The game's language exists to keep some fools out and trap even bigger fools in. You'll have heard of donkeys and fish, but what of the rockets? What of the fishhooks and gay waiters? What of the suck and resuck, the gutshots and wraps and double bellybusters? What space is there for a bad beat jackpot? What is there left to be said of tilt? Who is durrrr to you? What's an isildur1? How would you respond to OMGClayAiken? What is life before you've sharkscoped Spirit Rock, nanonoko, moorman1? This language is the soul of poker. Cards are but a blunt instrument. Cards are the messy, unpredictable side note to the sport. It is cards, however, which force the drama of life.

Internally, Martin is humming the Pink Panther theme-tune. This makes him feel sneaky.

*Da dum, da dum, da dum, da dum, da dum, da dum, da dum, da **duuuuuuum**, da da da da dum*

The regulars are here. In poker, your name doesn't matter. Martin is not a known entity in the room. Recognised by this point, maybe, but not known. A reputation in poker has both boons and pitfalls. It takes upkeep, but it can be very valuable if used respectfully. To gain a nickname is the true marker of a casino regular. On the table behind Martin, Terminator and Ice Cold are discussing Jacks.

If Martin cared about money, he might stand a chance of securing a very notable presence, the kind that wouldn't have any bearing outside of the room's $12m^2$, but counts for everything within them.

Taking his place in seat seven, Martin is internally choosing the fanfare to his entrance, and the theme music to his plays.

Galvanise (Push the Button) – The Chemical Brothers, 2005

Martin longs to see a man's eyes as his bluff is called, the castration and all it represents.

Ouch

The card room has its own time zone, its own smell. Retirement is a weekly occurrence for some of these men. This is a place like no other. For some, poker is job like any other; the same old grind in a different setting. It presents the same patience, the same boredom, the same repetition. There's nothing healthy about this behaviour. These men are not healthy. These men are not your friends. They are miserable, deluded and poor. To them, Martin is shrapnel in the poker explosion.

The phrase, '*If you believe there's justice in this world, try playing poker*' comes fully formed into Martin's head. He knows that if he doesn't write it down now, he is likely to forget it. It goes into his phone's notes as: '*If u believe theres justice in the world, dnt play pkr*'

Is this Martin's future? Surely the universe is subtler than to put a whole room of future versions of Martin in direct display.

Humans – made from 100% recycled material

Seat seven allows Martin to survey his opposition. Whilst some players like wearing sunglasses to make their reconnaissance discreet, Martin prefers to get a good look at the fuckers. He likes for them to know that he is on their case, that he won't be taking their shit.

Martin sympathises with the will of a man who can hold up Kings Cross armed only with an empty suitcase.

He has fought death and won

Twice

Life is a side note

It has been **mastered**

The thing in seat two is too ugly to possibly be human. He looks like a fairground mirror has permanently distorted him.

Picasso-esque

After two limpers, the thing raises to £12. Martin is his only caller, holding 8♣9♣.

The flop comes T7J rainbow. Martin has flopped the nut straight. He checks, staring deep into the space between him and the thing in seat two. It is checked back.

The turn is another Jack. Martin bets £35. To his surprise, the thing reaches for chips. He churns a raise between his amorphous digits, but chooses to flat call.

The river is an off suit deuce. Martin has around a pot sized bet behind. He measures out £60 in £5 chips and carefully slides them across the line. He gets insta-called.

His chest seizes up. The world spins · Martin sees the table from the bottom of a swimming pool· *Figures merge.* **Faces float**. It is warmandclammyandfreezing *and   he   can't   breathe   at   all.*

"*Jack Queen*," announces the thing.
Snap. What a donk. "**Straight**," Martin says.

You gotta lay them down to me. I'm qualified

The thing's expression collapses. More than ever, it is a collection of flaws and blemishes with spatterings of sensory materials. There's a nose in there. There's an eye tightening. Martin throws the dealer a £1 chip and stacks his winnings.

The thing is laughing in a foreign way. His laugh is watery and loose. It's in an accent to be ashamed of. The kind of accent cast as a villain.

One million

It is the kind of accent that should be hidden behind a football shirt, rarely seen in public. The noise comes from deep within the thing. Martin thinks of Jabba the Hut.

"You *shit* yourself at my call, boy," it says, "**Good** for you. A straight? **Good** for you, boy. I *like* you boy."

"Thanks," Martin says.

The Lyceum closes for twenty-four hours a year, on Christmas day. Boxing Day is the second biggest business day of the year for a casino.

Martin is imagining an action figure of himself, with real folding wrist actions. He imagines his smooth plastic crotch. His eyes glaze over.

He is playing as one with the cards.

Zen

Hitting draws, making laydowns. It is wonderful. Martin is at a state of inner peace. Inner peace feels a little sleepy. No-one would punch a man who has achieved Nirvana.

A diminutive Arabic man makes a three-bet on Martin's continuation bet. The fold feels ideal. It is part of a natural order. There is a flow to the game. Martin feels a desire to thank the man for being complicit in his destiny, for playing a role in his Karmic alignment with the universe and fate and the cosmos and stuff.

Luck is nothingness. Martin embraces the determinism of the cards. The fluttering riffles and hygienic washes: preserving chaos, inviting human participants in a call to order, to dance in the magnificent show of life.

Two cards slice towards Martin in a perfect silence. He gathers with the left, cups with the right and teases his thumb under their edge. Like little sluts, they reveal themselves in a pair, giving themselves over to Martin, willing slaves to his mastery. In disgust, they are returned to the muck from whence they came.

Now, the flop is dealt face up, each card wide open, exposing themselves to the universe. Three secrets spoiled. Three separate fates sealed in one narrow movement.

Chip stacks represent degrees of enlightenment. Martin is three hundred and fifty steps closer.

£320

£270

£130

Nothingness.

♠ ♥ ♣ ♦

Martin is treating himself to a taxi journey home. His cabby has introduced himself as Sam. Martin has made the amateur mistake of taking the seat next to him. Sam looks melted and swollen. Hair protrudes from every exposed area of his body. His accent is heavy and northern.

"So I've just paid two-hundred quid on shots for my mutt. Big lazy fucker he is. Round as anything."

Martin feels very aware of how many things are not in fact round.

"Who do you think the first person was to reckon pets were a good idea? Fucker must have been mad. How did he convince his family?"

Baths are not round. Dreams are not round. Clowns are not round. Books are definitely not round.

"'Hey, this Dog is going to be living here now.' 'Yeah okay, that sounds good.' Not fucking likely, eh lad?"

Martin stares straight ahead and laughs just a little, resenting their stillborn conversation. He has been separated from around two hundred pounds. He should probably be upset. Poker seems a far sillier investment than a ball shaped canine.

"What do you do then lad?"

"Urm, I don't really do anything."

"What do you want to do then?"

"Urm, I haven't really decided. For now, I'm sort of a professional poker player."

"Oh, yeah? How's that pay?"

"It varies. I don't know. It's not what I want to do. It's just a thing. I don't know what I want to do."

It occurs to Martin that might be a joke. Martin might be on reality TV or something similar. There's probably a camera in the corner of the taxi. David would have done this, wouldn't he? This is definitely the type of thing he'd do.

"Don't you feel bad about that, lad. Seems like it's more common to not know than to have any clear plans. People just fall into things, mostly. That's how I see it. Maybe us ones who don't know what they want are the only ones who reckon it's worth talking about, eh?"

Martin responds with another awkward titter. It looks like there isn't a camera. There's almost certainly no camera. Martin feels all the frustration of a trapped fly. He considers drawing in the window side condensation.

"Don't you agree, mate?"

Shit. Did Sam ask something? Shit. Say something vague. He mentioned talking, probably.

"Yeah. People tend to say things without thinking. Like, just for the sake of it."

"You're not wrong. It's those toffs who do all the talking anyway. Men are most conservative when they've got a bit of luxury. I'd prefer to waste my time than to waste my money."

Martin is struck by this string of eloquence. He looks up to the rear-view mirror. He can see Sam's reflection. His face is studded with pocks of beard. It looks as though it'd feel like braille. His voice crackles and spits like an open fire. It's sort of disgusting. Martin feels like he wants to punch the wisdom out of Sam. Somewhere around the kidneys would be ideal.

"I 'spose we can't blame 'em though, eh lad? My dad told me, 'If virtue's its own reward, who can blame a man for looking a bit further.'"

"I am hypocritical," Martin says, somehow drawn in. "I don't think it is so bad. It seems unavoidable."

Martin thinks about professionals who are younger than him. He feels resentful. Footballers, singers, all that rubbish. Attempting to comprehend their determination and ambition is frightening.

Fuck ambition

Sam's face twinkles with crusty bits of amber.

"You got to know what you think, I reckon. Seems to me like people have lost touch with their own thoughts. No one's got the impression of a bigger picture. It's like these Sat Navs: they'll only ever let you see what's right in front of you. Life don't work like that though, does it lad? Seems like everyone just wants a direct path to the right place."

Martin is home. He feels like a philosopher. He tips Sam £5. Sam smiles a shit-eating smile.

VI
♠ ♥ ♣ ♦

Martin is awake. He is sat upright in bed, on Gmail Chat with David.

"Have I told you about my inventions? Your dad should definitely back some of my inventions. Or all of them, whatever. I think I came up with a few in my dreams."

Martin's bed could comfortably fit three people. It could, but it hasn't. Martin sits in the centre; his legs are fanned like a rooted plant.

"Yes," Martin says, "Wait, maybe only one of them. I didn't know you had others."

His legs are absorbing comfiness from the 100% pure cotton.

Lovely comfy nutrients

"Right, my first idea - it's a new one, not really an invention, it's just an idea: I want to attempt to patent this thing somehow you see. I want to patent that experience where you're walking towards someone and you come close to each other, and then go to get out each other's way, but you both go in the same direction. In my experience, it might happen up to like

five times. I want to call that thing a 'David Moment.'"

Pat-tent

"I'm sure there will already be a name for that."
"How can you check if you don't know the name?"
David has spelt the word *name* as *mane*.

Cooooool maaaaane

"Touché donk. I don't think my Dad would be interested in supporting that one. He takes himself far too seriously to see the value in that kind of genius idea. Pitching it to him would be like Dragon's Den, but with just my Dad being a dick to you. What are the others? The other ideas, I mean. Are they the same kind of thing?"
David sends Martin a sad face and updates his Facebook status to tell everyone Martin is a dick.
"Right, get this. This is a jackpot idea. Dollar signs in my ***fucking eyes***, baby: answering machines on doorbells."
David adds a large block of dollar signs to this.

$$\$$$
$$\$$$
$$\$$$
$$\$$$
$$\$$$

Martin doesn't respond for a few minutes. He is looking for his phone. He feels sure that he heard it vibrating. He moves around his room like a ninja.

Heroes in a half shell, Martin power!

Martin comes back to find that David has added: "Also, I can cure hiccups. I should definitely be a millionaire for knowing how to cure hiccups."

"Sorry I lost my phone. I thought I'd lost my phone. I should have asked you to call it. That would have been much smarter. Haha, I just saw your status. It's true, I am a dick."

Martin joins the two girls who have already *liked* David's status.

2008

♠ ♥ ♣ ♦

Ste's Facebook status reads, *omg, 5 numbers on the lotto!!!!!* A forty-eight comment conversation has transpired.

This Tuesday, Martin is meant to be presenting a seminar on Wittgenstein with Ste. Martin strongly doubts that Ste will be part of this presentation.

It is plausible, but exceedingly unlikely that this could be a *frape* on Ste's Facebook. Ste has no history of being *fraped*. He's not popular or friendly or intelligent or attractive enough to warrant a *fraping*. *Frape* is indicative of a close, personal relationship. *Frape* is an act of love. Ste is just not lovable. Certainly not lovable enough to warrant such a novel and uniquely soul-crushing *frape*.

Martin predicts that Ste will have considerably more friends in the coming weeks.

The presentation will be fine. It'll be fine. Martin is sure that it will be fine. He tells himself that the Tractatus is a dirty little slut of a book anyway. Wittgenstein gives himself over to anyone smart enough to breach his rhythm.

Wittgenstein holds the title of most baller philosopher ever. Wittgenstein had retired at 32, announcing that he'd solved every problem in philosophy. Wittgenstein was so baller, that he was able to convincingly claim that even his own work had no meaning.

The comment thread has passed sixty unique language games. Ste's win will probably not even make the news. *Whereof we cannot speak, thereof we must be silent.* Who ever heard of a five number winner? The National Lottery website tells Martin that without the bonus ball, Ste is one of 311 individuals who have earned £1448 for their five numbers. Martin has never played the lottery. He's never needed to fantasize about money. About needing money. Playing the lottery wasn't an option before

this
point

Why is Martin feeling jealous? Why should he care? It's nothing money. Why has Martin already developed a fine tuned resentment towards Ste's windfall. Why should *he* be rewarded? Does anyone actually earn money any more?

It's not like that amount of money is even going to change anything. What can be bought with it? A new computer? A holiday?

A

new computer... A holiday...

More than anything, Martin feels annoyed. The kind of glee that Ste will get from £1448 is inaccessible to him. £1448 could never satisfy Martin. There is something about money that just won't ever be fulfilling. It's all a bit like an itchy eye: only to be experienced through a veil, through a cover. Never to be contacted directly. Too finely balanced, too perfect for the corrupting human touch.

(**£1488**)

(**£1488**)

(£1488)

(£1488)

VII

Martin is shopping. Shopping is happening, happening right now. This is what he is doing, what he needs to do. This is definitely what he should be doing. Right, shopping. Yes.

While navigating the high street, Martin is highly aware of his wallet. Sitting in his back pocket, the wallet is a second heart. The wallet is Martin's identity. The wallet carries the sum and total of his entire existence. The wallet is the determinant factor to all human relations. There is money in the wallet, money with presence, money that holds true meaning. The meaning is held in its weight, imposed onto each wrinkle of her royal profile.

Martin is thinking in fearful terms: constantly sizing-up the pickpocketing/mugging capacity of anyone in close proximity. The pretty girl in the sari doesn't seem too much of a threat, but that kid with the spots looks like he could be a right prick.

In each new space, Martin makes sure to obey proper shopping etiquette, paying attention to a variety of the store's fine products and wares despite his fixed intention to purchase a single item. If he had to pick, he would probably go for the green set of spoons. Yes, definitely the green.

In a 1 x 1m^2 changing room, Martin struggles to bring himself to try anything on. His own clothes have melted to his skin. Now, they are one. They hold a bond more eternal than love, stronger than hope. Martin's greatest fear is that someone will be watching/recording him, masturbating in a dimly lit security room to the tune of his young, supple limbs.

Sexy Martin

At the tills, Martin is overcome by an almost primal instinct to hunch the bulk of his meagre body mass in a paltry defensive effort over his unsheathed wallet. When paying by card, Martin will sometimes get his PIN wrong on purpose, just to confuse any fucker who might be considering him a potential victim for their complex, target based identity fraud scam.

After having made his purchase, Martin prepares for the worst, convincing himself that an emotionally crippling alarm will be triggered upon his exit. A barrage of anxiety collapses from every SALE sign. Martin's gait is somewhat spastic.

Back on the street, the day is full. Martin considers that he could part the waves of shoppers by running and screaming at them. Running and screaming. Running and screaming.

Martin's purchases are being put through the standard maternal scrutiny. His mother is tutting. She is pulling expressions that are making veins stand out on her neck. Her high personal standards demand 100% cotton and subtle designer branding. Martin feels very uncomfortable in new clothes. New clothes refuse to be obedient; they hang on him, slack and shameless. Each new outfit screams the outline of the boy underneath. Clothes are never quite the wingman that they promised to be whilst still on a hanger. If clothes aren't going to respect Martin, like fuck is he going to respect them back.

The outfits that he had accumulated through adolescence were simple, practical and malleable. When treated as a working unit, they made up a very adequate, functional array of basic materials for any skinny white boy:

- x 2 pairs of Jeans
- 10+ plain, non-branded t-shirts
- x 3 lightweight jackets/ x 1 coat / x 1 heavy jacket
- x 5 hoodies [with and without zips]
- x 2 pairs of trainers
- ~ 10+ polo shirts
- etc.

Martin knows that he is not an ugly man. Nor boy. Nor human. His posture, walk, grace – they carry the ingrown elegance of old money; money that would bury you to the waist. His cheekbones suggest an attractiveness that the rest of his face struggles to match. Martin's body is tight, not strong enough to rape anyone. He's all dressed up and going nowhere.

The new trousers still hold a little bit of static. It tickles around Martin's groin like some kind of filthy magic.

"They look wonderful, Martin," his mother suggests.

"What about them looks wonderful? I feel stupid. I feel like I look stupid."

"Just take the compliment, please."

Martin has started thrusting. He is attempting to rip the bottom of the trousers open.

The tingling has begun to feel sort of nice.

"Do you think that's appropriate? Really? Stop it now. This is not appropriate behaviour."

"I love you," Martin says, thrusting in his mother's direction.

"Are you on drugs? This is what drugs look like. You're on drugs. Drugs aren't a solution, Martin."

"What, even when they're dissolved in water?"

Martin's mother attempts to suppress a laugh by turning her attention to Martin's new winter boots. They have a lightning bolt down their side.

"What made you choose these? They were supposed to be appropriate for an interview."

"Lightning is cool, mum. I don't want to work in a place that doesn't appreciate the coolness of lightning bolts."

"You won't get away with this forever Martin."

"I am unstoppable," Martin sings in a deep, Eastern European voice. He takes off the tingle trousers and runs in circles around his mother.

VIII

♠ ♥ ♣ ♦

In the summer months, Martin's mother can often be found laying on the patio or terrace, ripening under the mediocre-warmth of a British sun until her cheeks are thoroughly rosy with the illusion of good health. She will soon return to pale. Light has a tendency to catch under the hairs around her jawline.

For now, it is winter. Her sanctuary is the effervescent kitchen, glorious in its double-glazed domesticity.

"*Martin,*" she beckons her son. "Why do I still get porno pop-ups when we're paying £30 a year for these anti-virus what-nots. Surely I shouldn't be getting pop-ups."

Martin: consultant for all things technological, philosophical and miscellaneous.

"I don't know, Mum. I am really busy at the moment," he shouts back from the living room. Martin is playing Snake on Facebook.

"*Will you be looking for a job today?*" she shouts.

"Too busy today, Mum. Maybe tomorrow."

♠ ♥ ♣ ♦

IX

Martin and David are playing the same nine-man $50 Sit 'n' Go. They are colluding by sharing their hands over Gmail. This behaviour would classify as a *major breach* of Full Tilt Poker's terms of service. Between them, they currently hold around 70% of the chips in play. They have reached the bubble: four people are left and three will be paid.

"I can't remember the last time I enjoyed gambling," David says.

"I can't remember the last time I enjoyed anything," Martin says. "Got JT off here btw," he informs David. A Ten high flop is checked round, allowing Martin to turn trips and shove to take down an average sized pot.

"Nice hand," David says.

"Thanks. I had trips. Got sixes now."

"You're running good."

"I always run good," Martin says, adding a winking smiley.

Martin does not always run good. No one *always* runs good. Almost no one. The flop comes King high and Martin insta-folds to a pot-sized lead from the big blind.

"I'm bored," David says. David has not played a hand in two circuits. When colluding, it is perfectly acceptable to let one partner do all the work. Martin and David had tried multi-tabling this venture, but it had proved too confusing. Plus, it would surely be more conspicuous. Surely?

"Link me to some good porn, Martin."

"What is good porn?"

"Never mind, got **AK** suited," David says. He ships it from under the gun and the small blind calls with nines.

"Folded 94o," Martin says.

Sweet as fuck

The board comes 4-4-**K**-3-7. They are in the money. Online, there are no apologies or awkward goodbyes. Martin and David are both now guaranteed $100.

"Nice hand donk," Martin says.

This sit 'n' go is part of Martin's infinite regress of distraction. Once he busts, he will descend another rung on the ladder.

David is a distraction from the Poker,
Poker is a distraction from the internet,
The internet distracts Martin from television,
Television distracts Martin from his parents,
who in turn prevent him from thinking

and thinking is the best way to avoid living. Martin feels aware that this logic doesn't reflect kindly on David.

"Dude check this out," David has sent a link to Eurogamer. Martin opens the link, which advertises a new videogame that involves shooting humans.

"Oi donk. You can't distract me mid-flow man. I'm in my zone right now,' Martin types, looking over the advertising anyway. "You wouldn't ask a porn star to stop mid-cum."

"What's a porn?"

2009

♠ ♥ ♣ ♦

Martin is in Kensington, Chelsea. His therapy sessions are priced at £165 an hour. Today, the topic of discussion was designated to be Martin's supposed 'fear of success'. Before each session, Martin takes some time to rehearse his problems, so as to seem sincere.

"I feel really aware of being pompous," Martin explains, rhythmically tapping a plastic bottle on the tip of his nose. "Like, *super aware* whenever I start to complain about something. I feel that I have no right to complain. If I compare my circumstances to any historical setting, or any other social situation, it seems clear that I couldn't have it any better."

Martin can feel the vibrations all the way up to his eye sockets.

"I feel like I am guilty of depriving another, more legitimate human from being part of the world; like I don't deserve it. Like, somehow, deserving my life should matter, or something. It seems too stupid that it could all just be down to chance - that I am the sperm of someone with a bit of wealth. It seems ridiculous that I have these opportunities, yet I couldn't give a fuck about them. People kill for the kind of life I have.

At least, I suppose they do. They almost definitely do. People can be relied on to do terrible things."

Dr. Henry Branton, PhD., Martin's therapist of three months, looks flatly towards him, making a controlled gesture that suggests he wishes for Martin to elaborate.

"I think I feel like I have to take actions to make up for the unfairness. The unfairness of the money, I mean. Like, I try to make myself a little realm of fairness in an unfair universe. I'd like to think that my actions can place some order into an otherwise random and *shit strewn* world."

Shit stew

"Like, when I scratch one side of my face, I feel a compulsive, soul motivated obligation to scratch the other side, just to even the universe out a tiny, little bit."

Dr. Henry Branton, PhD raises his eyebrows and re-crosses his legs.

"Your suggestions infer that you have been treating every part of life as a potential setting for therapy, Martin," he says. "I don't know how best to help a man who cannot stop acting."

"Thank you, Doctor," Martin says, knowing exactly what he means.

X

♠ ♥ ♣ ♦

"Who do you think it is that uploads videos to YouTube? Like, all the music videos with lyrics and pictures, all those non-official ones. Who uploads those shows from the 80s, dude? I don't get it. I don't think I'll ever get it."

"Maybe that could be our job. Not uploading the videos, but finding out why people upload the videos," Martin suggests. For a moment, he feels very serious about this suggestion.

Tonight on Panorama: Internet Altruism – The YouTube Story

"Reading that made me want to cry. I can't even remember the last time I cried. We are really fucked. If that's our best job option now, we are so fucked."

David sends a crying emoticon. Martin watches it a little while before replying.

"I haven't cried in the last six years, I don't think. Other than, like, those wind tears."

Gale force weeping

Today, Martin is making a list of the games he likes to play. So far, he has identified the following:

- Peeling labels
- Ripping up receipts into long paper strings
- Spitting from his window
- Putting CDs in his MacBook just to hear them spin and think about spinning that quickly
- Barking back at dogs
- Handing out bad beats like a boss
- Walking along the edge of pavements
- Thinking about biting off his tongue
- Thinking about what tattoos people might have hidden under their clothes

This list seems comprehensive. Martin thinks how happy it would make him for the list to be used as an itinerary at his next birthday party. Martin wonders if he will live to have another birthday party.

"Have you ever been in a fight?" asks David around twenty minutes later. "Fights seem very important. I would like to fight you and win. I think that would make me feel really good about myself. Knowing that I could hurt you. Not the actual part of seeing you in pain. I'm not a sadist."

"If you like, we could swear at each other over Xbox Live. It is really funny when white-trash kids are racist on Halo. Actually, we could fight on Street Fighter 4. That seems like something we could do as a legitimate alternative," Martin offers.

Tonight on Panorama: Halo Racism – No End in Sight

David does not reply for five minutes. Returning, he asks, "Does your head look too big? My head seems far too big when I am naked."

"Oh dude, have you been wanking while we were talking? Ewwww," Martin sends a series of laughing and gagging emoticons. As he selects them, his own face is perfectly neutral.

"Just kidding, it's okay," he says, sending a smiley face to show that David's masturbation would not bother him.

No hard feelings

"No I wasn't wanking. I will wank out of spite now. Spite wank."

Spwank

"Oh, I wanted to ask: how do you know if you are allergic to something? I'm either allergic to pollen or to people. My head is big because I am allergic to people and it has swollen up with their shit."

"Yeah, me too. Maybe it's infectious. Maybe you are seriously infectious."

"What should we do?" asks David, including a confused emoticon.

"We should kill all people."

"Okay, that sounds good."

XI

Thinking back, Martin cannot remember a reason for his second suicide attempt. There had been no explicit causal event or circumstance. There had been no trigger to the breakdown. And it was a breakdown. Categorically, it must be classified as a breakdown. All outward signs had pointed to Martin handling the depression. The initial suicide attempt was hardly spoken of.

The second was of a different flavour. The failure was more pronounced. When challenged, Martin had suggested that it had just felt like *something to do* on that day. Martin remembers the suicide as being a crisp, sharp thought. It had been a really good idea.

Cars have never charmed Martin. One car seems the same as the next. Despite Martin's father being a firm believer in public transport and eco-responsibility, his motor collection remains vast enough to be worthy of its own wing of the house.

Martin differentiated the collection by their faces. All cars have faces. The glaring headlights, the smiling number plates. A car's face can express everything.

Martin's selection of an appropriate suicide-vehicle was based on a cursory visual assessment of each machine's sturdiness. The more fragile, the better. Martin remembers having been truly pleased by this anti-logic. The settled choice was a standout winner. Its expression was extremely serious: taut, firm, cold. Plus, the vehicle was red, which naturally made it seem both fast and aggressive.

Grrrr

Keys were kept and left in each car's transmission. To Martin, this seemed to be asking for trouble. For one thing, it had shown considerably too much faith in the house staff. Elza would steal these cars in an instant. A mentally constructed image of Elza hot-boxing the family car has stayed with Martin.

Rebellion

Martin's plan (if it could be called a plan) was to take down the oldest tree on their grounds. Diameter: 1.5m. Age: old. The family's previous home had even older trees. Better, older trees. Trees with the kind of age that meant something. Martin feels confident that his name, initials and various expletives remain clumsily carved into some. He can clearly visualise his eye-level penknifed *TITS*. Martin is 60% sure that he had never made a spelling mistake on a tree. This detail seems significant.

Martin's funeral service was to be minimalist. Only flarf poetry would be read. Alternating songs by John Cage and STOMP would be played through the ceremony. It would be intense. Seriously, truly intense. Martin's aunt, his someone, would wail. His coffin would be made of polystyrene and adorned in affectionate graffiti. A full body cast. Martin would be buried with a deck of cards.

The ignition had mumbled, unsure of itself. Almost reluctant. The car had not been nearly so red and dynamic from the inside.

The tree, his final tree, was 100m away. A straight line. A final, morbid procession.

0 - *60* – ~~flatlined~~ in 20 seconds.

In the moment that Martin's life was supposed to flash before his eyes, a glare had caught him. His last thought was of sunglasses.

Rayba-

The bonnet crumpled like rice paper. Car wreckage has no discernable expression. Maybe agony? Martin had remained conscious for the crash. It had sounded like a million sheets of bubble wrap being horribly, sadistically twisted. The red car had been sturdier than Martin's estimation. Sometimes, he reflects on the final instant – the sunglasses and an all-too-human impulse to hit the break. That instinct should probably mean something. Anything. Right?

Paramedics had to cut Martin's body out of a seat belt. On sitting down into the driver's seat, he had unconsciously and automatically put on his seat belt.

During his suicide attempt,

Martin had been wearing a seat belt.

He'd never live it down.

He did.

Recovery was fine. Doctors mentioned that Martin had *good, strong bones*. A more serious consequence of the crash had been the parentally enforced ban on driving lessons. Since *the second episode*, Martin has learned to love the bus.

XII

♠ ♥ ♣ ♦

Sunday lunch dinner. Family time.

Martin pushes the remains of his meal around a bone china plate with a lazy satisfaction. He doesn't enjoy the metallic sound of his fork against the ceramic surface, but he feels a strong compulsion to keep it up, as though the self-torture were of some value. Martin has been gritting his teeth against the sound. He can feel the seed of a headache.

"Tomorrow is party night, Martin," his mother says. "Do you know what you'll be wearing?"

"No, not yet. A white shirt and tie, maybe? A white shirt seems like a safe choice."

Martin's parents hold annual *networking* parties in their family home. In theory, these parties are advertised as work related. Work justifies everything. Work permits the long-term neglect of a once brilliant son. On party nights, Martin's role is to be silent and smart. Aged eight, he was instructed to play the 'If I Speak I Will Die' game. It was a game to be taken seriously. Since then, he has grown into the habit of internally narrating the experience like a wildlife documentary.

Here, the suited leader eyes his prey. Her fur bodice is no match for his penetrating gaze. See how he lies in wait, weighing his moment, preparing for the strike. When it comes, her assets will be fixed into one premium bond. Then, her carcass will sit, torn open for the pack to feed

"A shirt would be fine. Just fine."

Party nights follow a safe script. Reception. Drinks. Dinner. Coffee. Routine dictates that Martin's father will greet guests by the door while his mother floats the floor, introducing strangers and their spouses.

"Jill is a copyright editor, and this is her husband Malcolm. He is a military technician."

"Kevin and Samantha have been married, what, ten years now? Kevin is the CEO of an international design house, and Samantha organises surveys for quiz shows."

"Francesca is engaged to Andrew. She's taking a break from her job in massage therapy to support Andrew's taxidermy ambitions."

Sitting at the table, grinding his teeth, twirling his fork, Martin is occupied by the overwhelming desire to ask: "Is anyone here happy?" He feels as though it is the only thought he has ever had. It plays on repeat endlessly through his mind. It plays loudly, over and through the emerging headache. The question is so overpowering that the answer is not significant. Martin makes no attempt to assess whether anyone is happy. No - this is a matter to be addressed and assessed vocally. Martin feels as though he cannot remember ever having spoken, as though he has forgotten how, somehow.

"Is anyone here happy?" he whispers.

"What was that, Martin?" his mother probes.

"Oh, nothing. Good potatoes, Mum. Thanks."

Martin's father appears to be on the verge of saying something tremendously important, but supresses it with a loaded fork of mashed potato. His cheeks pop out, thronged with age and broken capillaries. They are purple and self-pitying. Martin's face feels itchy.

"Do you remember when we made dinners together? I did enjoy when we made dinners together. You were quite the cook, you had an eye for it, or rather a tongue!" She laughs giddily. It is a contrite laugh. It drips from her. "Maybe we could get you an apprenticeship in a kitchen, Martin. You'd enjoy that, wouldn't you?"

"Yeah maybe, thanks Mum."

Looking over at the stern consternation ripped across his father's face, Martin knows he will never work in a kitchen. This conversation is for appearance's sake. Like charades at Christmas. Maybe that's okay, he considers. Maybe this is natural, normal even. Maybe this isn't so fucked. Hell, maybe being fucked is the norm.

On Martin's first train journey to university, his father had requested for an elderly gentleman to move out of their reserved seats in an otherwise empty carriage. This is the kind of man that his father is.

Martin has not had a fully formed conversation with his father since 2006, when he went through a self-conscious period, during which he tried to work off his teenage blubber. He would jog around Parliament Hill Fields running track whilst his father sat on a bench by the marquee, reading the Financial Times and shouting motivational clichés as Martin passed.

"Pump it!"
"Go on, lad!"

After a month of this routine, Martin's father conceded his lack of athletic prowess and Martin resumed smoking. The fat has since melted away. It turned out that stress was a good way to diet.

Then

out of nowhere

"It's just that, you've been spending an awful lot of money, Martin,"

Martin's chest has seized up. His neck is bristling. His legs have gone numb. His throat feels very dry. The headache swells to a high pitch.

"Your father and I do notice these things, you know. We have a meeting arranged with the bank manager on Thursday. We hope you don't mind. It's not that we don't trust you darling. Please don't think we don't trust you. It would just be reassuring to know where the money was going."

Martin may throw up over the table. He has begun speaking without realising it.

"Yeah, sorry about that, Mum. I still have it all, well, most of it. Sometimes, I like, take it out and don't spend it, then leave it upstairs and forget about it. I'll be more careful. Sorry about that. I didn't realise it was becoming a problem."

The transparency of the lie is dazzling, even as it is drooling out of him. He feels very hot and ashamed and needs to pee quite badly.

"May I be excused please?" Martin stands and leaves without waiting for a reply.

2009
♠ ♥ ♣ ♦

Martin has returned to university. People are being notably careful around him. His suicide attempt seems to be very much in the realm of public knowledge.

Today, Martin has been inconvenienced by a trip to Sainsbury's. The food-laden bag had pinched the skin on his palm a little. This was a fresh pain. This was the pain of the ordinary. This was a pain that all those pills couldn't reach. As Martin moves in public, he feels extremely self aware, like the feeling of a new haircut. Everyone looks at him, trying to identify a change.

At this moment, the most important questions in life seem to be:

1) Do you wipe sitting down or standing up?
2) Do fires really happen? Has anyone actually seen a fire?
3) How many different toilets will I use in a lifetime?
4) How many times do I tie my shoelaces in a year?

5) Are you supposed to use an equals sign or a semicolon when you create a Facebook emoticon?
6) How many Pringles do you have to eat before you get sick of eating Pringles?
7) Does anybody actually use bookmarks?
8) Does anybody actually click on pop-ups?
9) Does anybody actually pay for porn?
10) Why would you create a virus?
11) Who creates computer viruses?
12) Am I immortal?
13) Does anyone still use MSN Messenger?

Martin feels like a real philosopher when he considers these things. They are keeping him occupied. He has been thinking a lot recently. Conscious, logical thoughts. This seems positive. It seems affirming. Keeping busy seems vital right now. Martin has convinced himself that the daily impact of twenty cigarettes can be cancelled out with a solitary press-up and some internal reflection.

Martin is in the process of listing jobs that he cannot imagine people having or doing. The list does not yet seem comprehensive enough to sell to a magazine or academic journal. As it stands, the list looks like this:

1) YouTube Uploader
2) Pellet Gun Maker
    The concept of a weapon-toy hybrid seems startling, when thought about. Martin had wanted a pellet gun very badly when he was twelve. His parents

had flatly refused. Martin hid his
independently acquired purchase in his
sock drawer. Elza had found it within
three days. The pellets were yellow.

3) Drug smuggler

Martin had once thought out a
wonderful method of smuggling drugs.
The details are now hazy, but it had
definitely involved high profile,
internationally famous models.

4) Tattoo artist/Tattoo shop proprietor/Plastic
Surgeon

It seems startling to Martin that one
individual could handle the pressure of
inflicting a visible sign of commitment
onto another human in exchange for
monetary gain. Tattoos and cosmetic
surgery go some way to disproving
Martin's personal philosophy on how
humans are prenatally adverse to
commitment.

5) Carpenter/Blacksmith/Farmer/any kind of
primary industry based job

It seems ludicrous to Martin that
humans are still needed in the primary
sector. He hypothesises that their
continuing existence may well be a
good will gesture from the machines
before the final uprising.

Looking at the list, Martin feels exhausted. He has
earned a nap.

XIII

♠ ♥ ♣ ♦

Martin is outside, smoking. He is smoking and it is okay. Everything is fine. It is important to be calm. Martin pisses nervously into the darkest area of the garden, aware that some of his urine is being blown back at him. He is being splattered in himself. He doesn't care. He doesn't care doesn't care doesn't care.

FRANTIC INHALE

Martin has been smoking since he turned sixteen. At school, there was little else to do. Boredom breeds vice. At the start of his addiction, Martin spent around a month's worth of free periods practicing and perfecting his rolling technique beneath the wooden, penis-engraved study-hall desks.

Those boys who chose not to smoke were a deprived minority, to be pitied, not judged. They were the athletes and the asthmatics; by no means segregated, but always somehow lacking. Failing in that most vital of qualities.

gentle exhale

Martin had spent a considerable amount of time
refining the manner in which he smoked. It seemed
important, since smoking was a public and therefore
communal act. In essence, smoking is a performative
act. Martin's technique was centred on the pained
expression that accompanied his inhalations. When
smoking, Martin looks dramatic and troubled; he
suffers for his art.

FRANTIC INHALE

Feeling flushed and victimised, Martin is panicking.
They know. Of course they know. They must do.
Bank statements would list Full Tilt Poker. They list
the Lyceum Casino. I've got to stop, he thinks. I've
got to make it back, he thinks. Make it back, and then
stop. Then stop for good. Why did I tell them that I
had it? There was no need. I've totally fucked myself.
I'mfuckedI'mfucked I'mfuckedI'mfucked.

gentle exhale

Wasn't the lowest point meant to be a peaceful place?
Why hadn't they found out sooner? Why hadn't
Martin considered that they would find out? How had
Martin somehow managed to repress any conception
of consequences to his actions? Why had this not
occurred to him? Why does all this have to be fitting
together only now?

FRANTIC INHALE

Martin feels guilty. The guilt is an amalgam of all the negative emotions implicit to wasted talent and a deliberately-ruined-cherished-possession. His head aches in the kind of self-inflicted way that is hard to pity.

It reminds him of a time last year, when he had danced too close to a blaring speaker system, so as to seem manly to a girl he might have caught the eye of.

gentle exhale

A hundred different things seem to be occurring to Martin in a slow-motion-panic. It is the kind of panic generated by a toppling beverage during the minutiae before a [now] unavoidable disaster: the staining of the tablecloth, the fuss about the glass shards, the cries of an infant. His chest swells with a tension similar to an impending bout of hiccups. Martin scolds himself for not having asked David about his miracle cure.

D'oh

Martin needs a plan. He needs something. He'll take anything.

XIV

It is 4pm, Monday, night of the party. Martin is at the casino. He has not slept.

Every book about poker that Martin has scanned through, read or studied extensively takes a considerable amount of time to warn against doing exactly what he is doing right now. Even as he plays, Martin is fostering some serious cravings. Not cravings for money or nicotine, rather more pathetically, cravings for the next hand. Martin is presently committed to a persistent, cringe-worthy self-flagellating internal monologue.

I'mfuckedI'mfucked I'mfuckedI'mfucked

It is in these moments of stillness between hands that Martin's consciousness rears up most atrociously. Stillness allows thinking, and thinking is inexcusable. Thinking. The term seems disgusting, hardly real, barely a proper verb. Martin needs to be occupied, distracted.

The other players seem to know. Of course they know. These fuckers don't miss a trick.

He cannot bear this *thinking-thinking-thinking*.

Q. Since when does desperation make addiction more intense?
A. Since always, you fool.

Q. Since when has society been this dumbed down?
A. Since you felt the need to ask that question.

Thinking can only ever be de   stru   ctive.

Thinking implies a subject, and subjects demand legitimacy of attention over other subjects. It all seems so _{exhausting}. Martin's so sleepy. He's so tired.

Martin feels as though he is missing out on some divine poker secret when people take more than thirty seconds before making a lay-down or raise. Normally, he has decided what he is going to do well in advance of any move that his opponent might make. Sure, he plays along with the act and pretends to labour over some decisions, but it's not because of internal conflicts – it's for the pretence of the act. He simply can't find something in each action that's worthy of thinking about that carefully. Maybe that's where his problem is. Maybe that's why Martin's a 'losing gambler'. Maybe you need more than instinct to play poker.

Degenerate

Martin feels extremely jealous of people with a 'legitimate' addiction, the kind of addiction that he'd be getting sympathy for. He longs for an addiction that would generate a physical dependency and then have outwardly visible effects; the kind of addiction that is written about and problematized by the media.

You'll never see a beggar with a sign reading: **NEED MONEY 4 GAMBLING**. It just wouldn't garner any sympathy. People affiliate gambling with laziness. They comprehend the 'one-big-win' logic. They assume that is all a gambler ever wants.

Martin knows that some gamblers want to believe this also.

Right now, he is banking on waiting for *ACES - Bullets Baby*! He's praying for bullets.

Gambling isn't something you can trace a family history of. Martin would bet that it is hereditary. He would bet on anything.

In the casino toilets, there are pamphlets on gambling addiction. The pile never seems to diminish. The sinks are fitted with motion sensors that refuse to recognise Martin's hands. He is a gambling ghost with pissy fingers.

"I'm fucked," Martin reminds himself. This fact is getting stale.

This is in the realms of legitimate suicide material. This should make up for the previous times. He couldn't have been expected to go cold turkey though, right? That's not how recovery works. The

NHS should offer gamblers a three month free-roll. Hell, they might even make some profit.

There isn't even any camaraderie among gamblers. At least crack and smack addicts can sort of be co-dependent. For Martin, everyone that can be 'related to' is an opponent; they exist only in reference to his bankroll. Gamblers hate other gamblers with a passion. Martin thinks that all the action that goes their way is a direct curse from God upon him. And as for those donks who choose to call poker a 'sport', well, Martin doesn't know where to begin addressing their misjudgement.

Martin feels like he wants to make himself sick. "I am a human novelty," he considers, mucking K♠8♦ UTG +1. "Member of the most privileged percentile in Europe, I am here to amuse and delight '*others*' through justifying the legitimacy of their lifestyle choices in comparison to the abject failure of my own."

The man to Martin's right is the shade of light bruising. He has the unnerving qualities of a bald woman.

Between hands, Martin calculates that over the last five months, through his own gambling habits, he has lost between 2 and 2.5% of what he approximates to be his father's total wealth. He has exhausted all of his own finances and the private investments made in his name, all of the cash ISAs, savings accounts, private bonds and investments. His parents may not have access to this data before Thursday.

Martin has been seriously considering running away. He cannot comprehend a situation where he could be forgiven, or possibly make this up to his parents. Neither can he conceive of any circumstances that would justify running away.

Martin's chest aches with dull panic. His face expresses this as a prolonged and agonising pain. The prolonged and agonising pain takes the form of a smile. "This is very serious," Martin insists to himself.

The truth is this: every man wants to be good at poker. The romance of cards goes beyond the skill, the wit of the game. Poker is about much more than that. Poker is about judgment and conviction. Poker asks a man to back his read and be prepared to go all the way with it. Poker asks a man to stand by his judgment, present himself as an equal to anyone. Poker demands that a man should be prepared to play with something of value, something worth losing.

Martin doesn't know what's worth losing. It is 8pm and he dropped another £200.

♠ ♥ ♣ ♦

XV

This is no time for a taxi. Martin is on the bus, considering the possibility that his life might be more valuable than himself. Martin somehow feels transcendentally jealous of himself. He is floating around the roof of the bus, viewing the physical-ontological-Martin as a dick who he wouldn't want to be friends with - a dick who fucks-up and wastes other people's money. The moment seems noetic, ineffable, blugh.

Transcenfuckdal

Martin knows he doesn't want a job. He would be poor at whatever he did. Martin cannot imagine a feeling worse than being consistently reminded of how bad you are at something you have to do, something people are depending on you to do competently. Martin considers that a key to the problem is the proliferation of his choices. Martin has more job options than there are Mortal Kombat characters.

When people are brought up on a farm, and have a clear career path where they'll be a farmer, and are trained in how to be a farmer, they won't feel depressed about being a farmer, and there'll be little-to-no chance that they aren't going to be good at farming. But when you're privileged, you're indoctrinated with this illusion of freedom-of-choice, the idea that 'you can be anything you put your mind to'.

Martin decides that the worst thing about being Bill Gates is the inability to fantasise about what it would be like to be Bill Gates.

Martin remembers something from his degree called 'facticity'. Martin only understands the term in the framework of one reference, but if pressed, would roughly define his understanding of it as: being in a position with an abundance of choices to contend with, and the demand to select at least one.

Fuckticity

A child is pressing the bus bell repeatedly. The top deck passengers look in disapproving solidarity at the child's female guardian, who is busying herself with a tabloid newspaper. London is judging her.

RING   RING   RING RINGRINGRING RING

"Little son of a bitch."

Martin's father inherited a lot of money, and then had the audacity to make his own fortune in advertising. A while ago, Martin had thought he could follow this line. He has certainly inherited his father's talent for bullshitting. Martin got his degree off the back of bullshitting.

Phi-lols-ophy

Conversations with Martin's father are like a game of Jenga. Conversations with his mother are like a game of Guess Who. Life is like a game of chess. Poker is like a lesson about chess. Martin likes to play games.

On graduating, Martin returned home. He suggested to his parents that he wanted to volunteer for UNICEF, just for a little bit, while he made up his mind 'about things'. He imagined that being mechanical might feel productive; plus, there's no nasty, underlying cynicism to charity work: no overwhelming feelings of corporate resentment. Martin had thought that it might make him feel good, even if it were only for a little while, it would make him more of a real person, you know?

At present, Martin is seriously contemplating the idea of hitting a child.

B, B, A, Up, Right, B. "*FATALITY*."

Of course his father wouldn't hear of it. If Martin wanted to volunteer, he could volunteer to take Elza's job. He could volunteer to make some money.

Since the UNICEF incident, Martin has not bothered to share any of his equally noble ideas. Save the tigers. Save the children. Save the planet. Save the goal. Good intentions count for nothing.

Kitchen apprenticeship? They could fuck themselves.

The child continues.

RING RINGRING RING RINGRINGRIN-RING RIN GRINGRING RINGRINN NNNNGGGGGGGGGGGG

A suited man mutters something under his breath. Martin can discern the words 'ridiculous' and 'utter'.

"That's a fucking ugly child you've got there," Martin considers.

None of these people have faced death.

None of these people face uncertainty.

None of these people can fix this.

Martin has made it to the final table of Full Tilt Poker's Daily Dollar Rebuy Tournament. He has been playing for seven hours. During this time, he has smoked six cigarettes. He is playing solidly. His VPIP is hovering around a pretty looking 25%. First place would award Martin $876, a mighty good return on his dollar investment. Whilst not his biggest payday, this is already the highlight of Martin's online poker career. He is alone in his room at university. It is 4am.

At present, Martin's Sharkscope graph looks something like brainwaves in a seizure: it looks like the cross section of a psychopath's rollercoaster design. On average, Martin deposits $300 every week. Full Tilt are very obliging, providing an 'instant deposit' function to assist his habit. Depositing makes Martin feel dirty.

Filthy Martin

If Martin wins this tournament, he will be over $400 in the green for this month, and sitting pretty.

At five to the hour, Full Tilt Poker allows players a brief break. During these intervals, Martin runs through a three-step cycle of luck seducing ablutions:

1. He texts David with an update on his progress [Martin prefers to be locked out of social media whilst running deep in a tournament. It's all about concentrating right now]
2. While seated, he taps at the table in a constant rhythm. At present, he is beating out the William Tell Overture
3. He smokes a cigarette out of his bedroom window, sprays deodorant to cover the smell, then refreshes his thoroughly pulped chewing gum

Martin keeps his fingers in a concentrated steeple to demonstrate his attentive professionalism. He is serious. He is determined.

He is all in from the cut-off with Q♠Q♥.

He has been called by A♠K♣.

He is losing the flip.

He is eighth and out, earning $98, an hourly wage of $10.89 an hour.

Another tournament starts in four minutes.

XVI

"I don't think I can fix this," Martin tells David shortly after logging on, having just returned from the casino.

A minute passes before the reply pops through.

"When I hear my heartbeat in my throat, I feel resentful towards it. I see it as an annoyingly lazy drummer who gets tired, then gives up too easily."

"I am really fucked aren't I?" Martin says, reiterating.

"Yeah, probably."

The situation is making Martin pull an intense expression, similar to someone untangling headphones. This anguish is blugh.

"I'm a **good** person, David. I know that I'm **good** really. **Good** people can fuck up too, right? **Good** people fuck up all the time. **Good** people get forgiven, right? Shit man, if I run away, will you drive me there?" Martin requests.

"I dunno, man. Will he really be that pissed? Wait, drive you where?"

"I don't know. It has to be tonight though. They'll be too distracted by the party to notice me leave. There will be lots of cars about. It doesn't matter where we go. I feel like there should be an app for this. Maybe that could be our invention, a destination generating app."

"brb, dude, I gotta smoke," David says.

Martin is hitting the random article generator on Wikipedia, hoping to find somewhere, anywhere in the UK worth running to.

♠ ♥ ♣ ♦

If he tells them, if he attempts to explain, then it might work a little like a guilty plea, Martin hypothesises.

He might receive a lighter sentence.

They'd be disappointed, angry, frustrated, yes.

But this way, they can't cut him off.

This was no worse than the suicides.

Not really.

He was being open with them: honest, like they'd taught him to be, like they thought he already was.

Martin wouldn't say he loves them.

Not more than any sense of obligation entitles him to.

Is that so awful?

It is probably awful.

He just doesn't love them in the important, biological way that other people seem to know about.

"Dude they don't hate you," David types. "You should see my parents. Stalin receives more sympathetic portraits than I do from them."

Quit Stalin

"I am Stalin, hear me roar."

"You're keeping your humour, then."

"No. I really am Stalin. I am the resurrected anti-Christ. I am the talisman of Communism. I pull the heads off kittens and play keepy-uppy with their skulls."

"What time do you want me to pick you up?"

"Give me an hour."

Martin's descent downstairs is plodded, like a death-march. He moves in a 4/4 time signature. He is going to do this properly. He is doing this on a full bladder.

♠ ♥ ♣ ♦

Martin's father has been aggressively berating him for the last twenty minutes. He stands across from Martin, inclined over the polished-oak dinner table in a simian posture, supporting himself with clenched fists. Occasionally, flecks of spittle are expelled from his mouth, just missing Martin. The party is due to start in an hour and Martin's father is dressed in an intimidatingly expensive suit. Thus far, Martin has played a silent role in this dialog. He had paid attention and felt very serious for at least ten minutes, but for what he approximates to be the last five, he has been thinking about how odd it feels to chew popcorn.

Poopcorn. Shampoop

"It's not normal what you do, boy. You think it's normal? Sitting in your room, doing God knows what? Chatting to all those online friends. That's not a life. That's not the life I've provided for you, boy. That's not what your mother and I have worked for. You could have been anything. You've wasted it all. You know what other boys would do for what you have? *You know how lucky you are?* You should feel ashamed. *You're a disgrace,* you know that?"

Now that it is out, all the guilt, panic and hectic energy that had surrounded him have

co

lla

psed

into a benign ache around Martin's lower spine. By Martin's reckoning, this is a 'no way back' moment. From this point onwards, he is eternally fucked. He briefly considers the possibility of this having the potential to become something liberating, something affirming, novel worthy.

This is a turning point. There is no lower Martin can fall. There is no one he could let down any further. Except, maybe if he suddenly became gay, but that just seems silly.

"Let's test the water," Martin thinks.

"You ought to be a little more forgiving to a boy with suicidal tendencies," he declares as his father catches breath.

"Don't you threaten me boy; don't you **dare** try to fucking threaten me." Martin's father's face vents a tame frustration at having being outwitted by his only offspring.

At this point, Martin stands. He begins to return to his room.

"That's right, run away you little **fucking** *coward,"* his father calls after him.

Okay, dad

Without thinking, Martin begins to pack a bag. He feels important as he does this. Each object in the bag is imbued with a profound significance, chosen above all others, chosen as part of Martin's new life. Items in the bag so far include:

- ☐ One packet of cigarettes [half empty]
- ☐ One toothbrush
- ☐ One tube of toothpaste [even cowards should have good oral hygiene]
- ☐ x 5 condoms [even cowards should be sexually responsible]
- ☐ x 5 pairs of underwear
- ☐ a pair of sunglasses
- ☐ a Richard Yates novel

"We need to go now," he texts David.

Martin's father is standing in his doorway.

"So you're running away? That the plan? Think you're a big man now, Martin? Think you can cope without my money? We'll see how you fucking cope. You can't last without me, boy. You haven't got the brains that God give a goose. You want to rebel against everything you are? Feel free. You want to escape? You can get the fuck out, because you'll *never* escape yourself boy. You're a failure. Simple. You're always going to depend on me. I've accepted that. But you fucking dare to come and make out like *you're not to blame?*"

Martin continues packing in an attempt not to listen. Each time he remembers something easily forgettable (medication/phone charger/hair brush), he feels strong senses of determination and independence. His stomach feels like a mechanical sound, like a stick bouncing off of railings.

- ☐ Phone charger
- ☐ Medication
- ☐ Vitamin supplements
- ☐ Empty water bottle
- ☐ Deck of cards
- ☐ Poker Chips

"Your problem is that you've got no problems, boy. Your life is so easy that you need to make it seem bad. You're creating problems – internal conflicts. I think you're trying to get yourself into trouble. You not getting enough fucking attention from us, or something? *Are we such bad parents*? So you need to suffer, I get that. But sometimes you need to be put in line, just like everybody else. A reality check will be good for you boy. You can fuck off for now, and I'll still be doing just fine when you come crawling back."

David has replied, saying that he is on his way over. It will take David around ten minutes to arrive. Martin ponders the need to bring his house keys. He decides it wouldn't do any harm to bring them.

- ☐ Deodorant
- ☐ Umbrella
- ☐ x 5 pairs of socks
- ☐ x 5 t-shirts
- ☐ The new, tingly trousers
- ☐ Jeans
- ☐ x 2 jumpers
- ☐ x 3 vests
- ☐ one hoodie

The bag is starting to get heavy. Martin considers saying goodbye to his carpet stain. The carpet stain is his whole life's work. Leaving it behind seems significant.

Freedom, lol

XVII

♠ ♥ ♣ ♦

Martin has just stepped into David's car (which is green with a serious face).

"This feels like a holiday, but better," David says.

"I don't understand the point of holidays," Martin replies, "It's just you, thinking your shit, in some other setting. You can't really escape yourself. All the same problems will still be there when you get home."

It takes a few seconds before Martin realises the depressing hypocrisy of this statement.

"We ain't never going back," David says in a dumb voice, turning out of Martin's driveway.

"Like, people are always longing for these chances to 're-invent' themselves, but it's all bullshit really. People can only act for so long. They always slip up eventually. It only takes one slip-up, and all the shit comes toppling down on top of you."

"I would re-invent myself like a boss. I'd be a fox. I wanted to be a fox for a while when I was younger. Foxes have a sweet ass life. No one fucking messes with a fox. Plus, they get to sleep all through winter. That's awesome. Foxes are awesome. Most animal lives are pretty sweet, but Foxes eat meat and shit."

"Yeah, they're good," replies Martin, switching on the radio.

Martin considers his place in a generation that instinctively knows how to handle the complexities of a car dashboard.

"Have you ever hit a woman?" David says.

"What? Where did that come from? No. Not yet anyway. I so would though. It seems like something that I will inevitably do."

"You are such a dick. You didn't even think about it. You didn't even really think before you replied."

"So somehow I'm less of a dick if I think about it? How does that work? That's not fair. That doesn't seem fair at all."

"I dunno, just seems like it's something worth thinking about. Like it should depend on circumstances or something. You could pretend you wouldn't at least."

"So you wouldn't?" Martin asks.

David's stubble is long and fine. It looks like a frayed shoelace.

"I sort of promised that I never would."

"Promises count for nothing. How can you keep a never-ending promise? It's like a life choice. That's a lifelong commitment you've got there. That's bullshit, David."

"Yeah. It's the sort of thing that I feel I can legitimately commit to though. If there's ever like a proper promise you can make, it should be something about how you treat people. That's the stuff Jesus discussed, isn't it? That is popular, man. People really do live like that. People like being forgiven, I reckon.

They need to know they can move on from anything. Christianity is good for that, feeling good about yourself, you know?"

Our Father,
Who art in heaven…

Martin doesn't know how to reply. It seems true. It seems very true. They listen to the radio for a while. Generic pop is playing. Martin is aware of knowing the words, and resents himself a little. Without realising it, he has begun singing along and David has joined him at the chorus.

"California Girls are unforgettable/Daisy Dukes, bikinis on top/Sun kissed lips, la la la la unforgettable/Wooo oooh-oh-oho-oh-oho-oo."

Martin smiles broadly. "I think that it's all going to be okay."

"I told my parents I was going on an adventure. They didn't seem bothered," David informs his friend.

"That is so standard."

"So, where are we going?"

"Wait, I don't know. I thought you knew. Where have you been driving? Where are we? Shit."

Ahead of them, the motorway moves heavily into the horizon like an endless accomplishment. Birds perch on redundant phone-boxes, lining the roadside every half-mile in wasteful persistence.

2009

♠ ♥ ♣ ♦

Martin is working as an intern at The Guardian.

A man also named Martin is managing him. Responsible Martin has a tubercular wheeze and constantly appears to be exhausted. With a big dumb smile, he informs his new employee that emphysema is 'so hot right now.' This could easily be the kind of joke that he tells three times each week. Martin imagines that this is the kind of man who might collect very fragile and cheap things that require regular dusting.

Intern Martin is conducting a master-class in procrastination. It is a skill that he perfected in school. His logic suggests that so long as he paces around the second floor office space at a reasonable pace, looking attentively around and carrying something fairly weighty, he will remain undisturbed. Martin feels smug as he achieves this. It occurs to Martin that everyone else may be doing the exact same thing.

Matrix

In the men's toilets, there are mirrors on both sides of the sink area. Martin looks deep into the simulated infinity, pulling serious expressions by overlapping his bottom teeth with his top lip and furrowing his eyebrows. No one else comes into the toilets. Martin considers smashing something. Instead, he makes a smashing motion.

Intern Martin has been assigned to copy-check a medical article. It discusses whether organ donation should be made into an 'opt out' choice, rather than something you have to actively commit to. Intern Martin thinks he is an organ donor. Responsible Martin had mentioned that he would allow everything but his eyes to be donated. Martin chose not to challenge this, but internally shouted

RETARD.

Intern Martin had accepted the placement hoping the myth that '*every female member of staff wants to fuck the work experience boy*' might hold at least an element of truth. The only female connection that Intern Martin has made so far today was when a suited Asian lady handed him a pen that he might have dropped on purpose. It had been an indistinct drop. It was among the top five vaguest pen drops of Intern Martin's life. Intern Martin couldn't imagine the Asian lady without her clothes on, despite trying quite hard for a little while. It seems inappropriate to look at porn whilst in The Guardian's offices. Martin mentally lines up a porn playlist for the evening instead.

Filth

Over the next two hours, he manages to fill two sides of an A4 sheet of paper with doodles including but not limited to:

- ☐ A cube
- ☐ A penis
- ☐ The 'super' S
- ☐ A spider
- ☐ A jellyfish
- ☐ A monkey with a jetpack
- ☐ A tally chart of Responsible Martin's visits to the bathroom
- ☐ The Pepsi logo (though it could pass off as a Yin/Yang symbol)
- ☐ The outline of his hand
- ☐ A stick-figure Responsible Martin hanging from a noose with wavy stink lines coming from the top of his head
- ☐ A badass gun
- ☐ A cross hatched heart
- ☐ Many spirals

Intern Martin decides that he will take this sheet home. His idea is to scan it onto his laptop and put it on Facebook in an album titled: 'My day at work.' This seems like a really good idea.

Responsible Martin has announced his intention to go to a driving range in around half an hour. The team of staff around Intern Martin pay no attention to this news, keeping neutral facial expressions while Responsible Martin lays off some practice swings with a ghost club into their workspace.

RETARD

XVIII

♠ ♥ ♣ ♦

"Craig's Facebook says he's ill," Martin reads from his phone.

"The only reason to let people know you're ill is to excuse yourself from something. Illness means excuse to me. Illness can almost seem like a good thing, something to show off about. Maybe Craig is showing off."

"I dunno. It could be evolutionary. Him telling us, I mean. Altruistic sort of. It's like a leper's warning. Preservation of the species, that kind of stuff."

David turns off into a service station to fill up their gas. Martin points out that if they want to seem cool, it'd be a good idea to turn off *Rio* by Duran Duran, which is playing on the radio. David concurs.

There are four free pumps. An elderly man is scolding himself for breaking the twenty-pound mark on pump six. Martin can see him aging three years in the process.

"So what's our policy here? Are we taking a defiant position where we refuse to use your dad's money?"

"I haven't really thought about it. I've never had my own money. We wouldn't get very far without using his."

"But, wait. What are you trying to prove? I thought you were showing him that you could survive without his money? I guessed that much any way."

"I never said that. Shit, I haven't thought about this. Running away is as far as I have planned."

"Well, why don't we set a limit? Like, we'll say we're allowed two-grand, and we'll see how far that takes us?"

"I don't feel like I'm achieving anything by doing this, David. This just feels dumb. Maybe I should go back. There doesn't seem much point to this."

"So? Let's keep going, just for a little while, to make it at least seem like we've achieved something. Maybe there doesn't have to be a point. Maybe we're just seeing what we can get away with. That's what life is, dude – seeing what you can get away with."

"No – you're thinking of art."

"Oh yeah. Well, it sounds good anyway."

"Yeah, okay. That does sound good."

David steps out of the car to 'fill it up'. Martin's phone starts ringing – it is his mother.

"Shit, David. My mum is calling me. What do I do?"

"I dunno, answer it?"

"But I'm running away. I feel like if I'm running away I shouldn't be answering my phone."

"Just answer it, Martin," David tells him firmly.

"Hello," Martin says, answering.

"What took you so long to answer?"

"I wasn't sure if I wanted to."

"Where are you?"

"I am running away."

Martin ponders the possibility that it was his sub-conscious knowledge of the futility of his present course of action that had prevented him from bringing his passport on the trip.

"No, where are you?"

"That isn't important. I am running away."

"You're being very childish, Martin. What are you hoping to prove?"

More than once, Martin had spotted his mother undressing identity from her finger. She had twisted the ring off, shaken her hand out, and then twisted it straight back on.

"I don't know. I feel like running away is my only option right now. It feels good so far. How is the party going?"

"Never mind the party. I don't like this at all. You're being very selfish. Your father is worried about you."

"Really? He's worried? In the middle of the party? Why would he be worried about me? What did he say?"

Martin doubts that his father is worried. Loving sentiment is not easy to detect. Metal detectors are not set off by marks of loving sentiment.

"He hasn't said he's worried, but I know he is." Martin's mother laughs a little.

"You're not taking this seriously," Martin scolds her.

"Neither are you! How can I take this seriously when you don't even know what you're trying to prove to us?"

Martin notices that David is reaching for his packet of cigarettes. He gestures wildly to get David's attention. David mouths out *What?* raising his hands to signal confusion. Martin mimes back a lighter action, then an explosion. Martin imagines that he looks like an improv stage actor. David slaps his forehead and walks around the corner away from the gas pumps. Martin's mother continues to speak.

"I just saved the world," Martin explains.

"Well done, sweetie," she says.

XIX

Martin and David are cheating the sun, *just* managing to keep hold of its edges by
incrementally
narrowing
margins
as it endeavours to escape from them.

Their trip has been headed north for a few hours now. They have just reached Birmingham.

"I like that we are being environmentally indulgent," David says, winding down his window.

"*Fuck the environment*," he shouts. His defenestrated wisdom catches the wind and shoots off behind them.

"I don't feel very liberated," Martin says.

"It feels misleading to say that we are '*running away*'," David says. "Can you really '*run away*' while sitting down?"

"This does feel easy. Running away should probably be harder than this."

"When was the last time you did something hard?"

"I don't remember. Life seems hard. Getting out of bed seems hard."

Martin is almost asleep. Road signs have begun to seem like lazy metaphors, communicating the pointlessness of their endeavour.

SLOW DOWN

GIVE WAY

DEAD END

ACCIDENT AHEAD

STOP

"I think we should stop for the night, dude," he suggests.

"We're nearly in Birmingham. We can hang out there."

"Sweet. I've never been to Birmingham before."

"I think I've seen more of France than I've seen of England. That seems fucked," David says.

"How was France?"

"I don't even remember. Good I guess. London seems better. London always seems better."

"Je mapple Martin. Jame le poisson et le poolet."

"Nice."

XX

♠ ♥ ♣ ♦

Martin and David are sharing a £25-a-night room in a layby Travelodge on the outskirts of Birmingham. They had requested a twin room at the front desk. The receptionist was a beefy, European looking-lady with a large mole just below her bottom lip, which had scared Martin.

Stepping into their room, they see that there is one double bed. The cover sheet is the many shades of a clown's vomit.

"Go and tell her that this isn't what we wanted," Martin says.

"Dude, I've been driving all day, you should do it."

"No, she scares me."

Martin imagines the receptionist's name is Helga. She likes to arm wrestle and puts cigarettes out on her neck.

"Well she scares me too!"

"Well I guess we're going to have to sleep in the same bed."

"Well I guess you're right."

"We could have got separate rooms you know."

"Fuck. Why didn't we get separate rooms? We're stupid. You're stupid. Why did that not occur to us? This is so gay."

Martin has not used a computer in over twenty-four hours. This seems significant.

The room looks like it should be either a crime or porn scene. Martin feels stubborn and childish.

He has not masturbated in two days. This seems significant.

"This seems really gay, David," Martin says as he climbs into their bed. The sheets crackle like terse plastic.

"Dude you're not supposed to say how gay it is. We both know it's gay. Admitting it out loud just makes it seem like we're choosing to accept how gay it is."

Below them, David's car braves the weather, its windows glazed with frost. The car park tarmac is iced over, fractured into a connect-the-dots pattern.

"I've been awake so long. I'm not used to this. I ration myself to ten hours of daylight a week, Martin."

A sinister looking crack travels down from the ceiling to behind the headboard of their shared bed. The room has the yeasty smell of sporty teenagers. A patch of damp decorates both corners of the room's far side. Martin is unfamiliar with reality at this intensity.

"Why do you think they only put sign language over shows after 2am? Are deaf people nocturnal or something?" Though this seems like a joke, David has not delivered it in a 'jokey' way. Martin consciously chooses not to laugh, and for it to be the last thing said before they sleep. He doesn't fancy the pressures of a formal 'goodnight' shared with a man sleeping next to him.

Martin plays with the thought bubble of hair below his navel until he falls into the gayest sleep of his life.

Martin is in an Ethics seminar. The class has been running for an hour and a half. Currently, Martin is deeply occupied with the thought of how his class would pair up to repopulate the world.

"Martin," his professor says, interrupting. "What do you think?"

"About what, sorry? Sorry."

"Absolute evil; the possibility of an absolute ethical maxim. Is it plausible that we can identify something as intrinsically bad?"

Martin thinks carefully. "I don't know. Racism, maybe? Papercuts?"

Jenny laughs hard. She had been paired with Owen, but Martin may have to reconsider this match. He sizes Jenny up for a wedding dress, a terraced house, a Vauxhall Astra, a Rottweiler, a son – his son.

"Well, pain, certainly is the primary evil of utilitarian ethics. But what flaws are there in qualifying evil by pain? Surely some individuals will have different conceptions of pain; different thresholds. And what of psychological pain? The pain that can't possibly be quantified."

It is a class of fifteen. Kenny Wallace is going to have to wank himself into extinction.

"How is pain symbolised in art? How do we figuratively begin to imagine pain? What symbolises pain for you, Martin?"

"Money," Martin replies.

Martin is awake. David is sat at the end of their bed, picking at his feet. His back boasts a single, spindling hair. As Martin sits up, they exchange a look: the sort of early morning gaze familiar among teams of manual labourers.

From the east window, a harsh barcode of light scans through the blinds, betraying the illusion that it might still be acceptable to roll over, back to the safety of sleep.

So shleeeeeepy

Martin lurches to the toilet, using his stream to clear anonymous skid marks from the bowl. Above him, the ceiling squeals. Martin imagines a mild mannered Asian couple falling through his ceiling, dressed in sharp creased pyjamas. He would fan away the debris, laugh politely, shake their hands, introduce himself and offer to call the front desk.

In the shower, Martin makes his fingers cry. They are a string of half-hearted waterfalls. Hooking an arm over his back, he washes in a windscreen wiper motion.

"Yeah," he thinks.

♠ ♥ ♣ ♦

Martin and David are taking a walk. Around twenty
minutes of their morning had been spent listing
possible activities that they could do for free.
'Exploring' was deemed the best choice. Just the word
was exciting, full of potential. This would be the real
start of their adventure –

they were going out

to

explore.

So far, the reality has been significantly less
glamorous. It feels as though they are just walking.
They are in fact, just walking. As they move, Martin
runs an empty Lipton Iced Tea bottle along a railing to
his left. The bottle pops and clocks over the iron,
stressing against Martin's wiry fingers. Martin spots
David looking jealously towards his bottle.

Mine. My bottle

"Can we stop? Let's just stop. Let's go in here. It's
too fucking cold."

A bell tinkles as they enter *Coffee Lounge*, but no
one looks up.

"Get me a coffee. When you order, ask that lady
something crazy," David says, gesturing towards the
middle aged black woman behind the café counter.

"I'll have a large English Breakfast tea and a large Decaf, please. And if you could punch anyone, who would it be?" Martin says.

"That's £4.20, please. What was the second thing?"

"Oh, I just asked: if you could punch anyone, who would you punch?"

"That, outside," she says without hesitation, chin-gesturing through the shop window, towards a tatty looking busker. Martin turns to look. He cannot recall having seen a busker on their way in.

"His name is Simon. Every day, the same songs. You don't know how sick I am of that man's voice."

"I'm going to talk to him," Martin says. "I'm on an adventure and Simon will be my new trampy friend."

♠ ♥ ♣ ♦

Simon says that he is on a break; he is not taking requests. A splintered guitar sits beside him. He swigs deeply from a can of lager, tilting his neck back to an obtuse angle. Drinking is part of his performance. The movement exposes a tatty scarf, hanging like a bib from his bristling neck. Were you to listen hard enough, you could almost hear the follicles grow. Simon is very French. Frenchness oozes from him.

"Ooze," Martin thinks, smiling broadly.

"And what is it that you do?" Simon says after they have been formally introduced.

Martin cannot think of a convincing lie, and concedes that he doesn't really 'do' anything. He explains that he is running away. Simon laughs deeply, jiggling his lager soaked belly.

"You do nothing. I do nothing. This is good."

Simon explains that he is known to officers-of-the-law. He calls himself a 'serial offender'.

"They see me pee here. They see me pee there. They say, 'Simon, please do not pee.'"

Simon picks up his guitar and begins playing as they talk. He explains how the police eye him with familiarity, perhaps the occasional (discreet) nod of kudos.

"I am a citizen. I am British. I am part of this nation."

During his degree, Martin had learnt that the job of a state is to protect its citizens.

Simon's medley is regular. He strums spritely pop tracks, spicing them with a life-affirming introspection. He explains that it is important for a busker not to seem needy, 'spare change' is a misnomer after all. No change is really to spare. His cardboard placard reads, 'Donate to the Arts'. Busking isn't charity. Simon offers a service.

Martin considers that busking seems a more professional occupation than writing.

"I'm not really here, you see," Simon says, hiccupping. "I am no one to them. I am, how-do-you-say, furniture on their periphery." Simon stumbles over the end of 'periphery' a few times, before pronouncing it triumphantly. "A feature of their day, I am - regularity; I am levelling to their lives. They do not ask, 'Sitting on the street every day, waiting for death, is that all there is?' They would not dare. I am a personal holocaust. I am murdered *over* and *over* by their stares, their how-do-you-say – objectifying inattentiveness. They cannot bear to admit being complicit in allowing my suffering."

David brings Martin his tea and returns inside, flashing him a concerned look.

"These people," Simon gestures. "They donate to charity and they feel good. They are, how-do-you-say, deferring responsibility to its proper representatives. Those more equipped to deal with my 'type', the likes of me. They will feel pure nothingness when I am gone, when I die and rot. They will lack me and not know what, why, who. I will be more powerful in my absence than I have ever been in my being. That shall be my legacy."

"Simon is funny," Martin thinks.

Martin attempts to explain to Simon how he feels guilty about almost everything, how the world seems to be his responsibility. Martin articulates how he grasps onto life with a sweaty grip, and the uncontrollably shaking hands that he has inherited. Simon listens passively, playing and seeming very occupied by an indistinct middle distance, which is inaccessible to Martin. Sometimes Simon nods, almost apologetically, taking breaks to sip carefully from his can, imbuing it with a bottomless mystique.

After a cigarette length pause, Simon tells Martin he's full of shit.

"Do you know what it is to starve?" he says.

"No. I imagine it is bad."

Simon smells of Elza's car.

"It is the most natural thing a man can do. To fast, to starve – it is to reconnect with the body. When you distance yourself from your mind, you may become a new self."

"You're full of shit," Martin tells Simon, offering him a fresh cigarette and standing up to leave.

"Wait, no, give me some money," Simon says. Martin laughs assuming that it is a joke. Simon stares back with a serious facial expression and an extended hand.

"I see through you, boy."

"Hypocrite," Martin mutters, walking back to David.

"What happened?" David asks, looking tired and impatient.

"Nothing, really," Martin says.

Martin has decided to quit smoking. He is quitting smoking. This time he is sure of it. This is the first true, real, genuine attempt. This will be the only attempt. This is the one that will count. This is the attempt to end all attempts. This is quitting.

Martin is quitting and it feels awful. It feels like he is resigning from some wonderful, ephemeral occupation. Why is it that every other form of quitting is frowned upon? Quitting is classed as 'giving up'. Quitting a team. Quitting a marriage. Only in this case could Martin receive plaudits for abandoning these twenty dear, fond friends; these gentle comrades. Shouldn't there be shame? Grievous, horrible shame? No. There is no shame. There is never any shame.

There goes his last butt, down to the dirty, fag strewn pavement. With a twist of the toe, Martin is severing a physical and spiritual bond. The butt sits there, mutilated. Martin exhales.

Nineteen doesn't seem old enough to have conquered a serious addiction.

Hours pass.

Now

his chest is tensed up and

sha

king,

ringing like a phone. It is all so Irresistible.

Overbearing.

He's out cold. Where are the **tar lips**? Where is the burnt breath of nightclubbed kisses? Where are the

proud smoking rants? When will there be space for free verse beatnikking?

Martin holds out his hands.
Five trembling cancer digits.
Tumour scissors.
Ten fallen warriors.

Four browned allies.

Days pass.

Martin's wallet is heavy with coins, the residue of addiction.

Tobacco. It's even fun to say.
So fine. So varied.

So exquisitely............*something.*

What of the casual dependence and midnight feasting in a social love-in among old friends and old strangers and complete failures and four activists and hypocrites and hypochondriacs and serial quitters and serial murderers and homeless company who wish the worst upon you?

Each *burn* was worth it. Each burn was nothing. Never memorable enough to justify. Never memorable enough to write.

After all, *emphysema is so hot right now.*

(RETARD)

Avoiding the worst was the worst that could happen.

And now it's all over and any time left is only for regretting.

There's a new addict in town.
(resist)

Duty free will   *never*   **be**
        the   same.

The economy will coll
                    apse   without   tobacco-fuelled
        custom.

Smoke   Smoke   Smoke
Smoke   Smoke   Smoke
Smoke   Smoke   Smoke
Smoke   Smoke   Smoke
Smoke Smoke _{sex} Smoke
Smoke   Smoke   Smoke
Smoke   smoke   Smoke
Smoke _{sex} Smoke Smoke
Smoke   Smoke_(resist)Smoke
Smoke   Smoke   Smoke
Smoke   Smoke   Smoke
Smoke   Smoke
SmokeSmokeSmokeSm
okeSmokeSmokeSmoke
Smoke   Smoke   Smoke
Smoke   Smoke   Smoke
Smoke   Smoke   Smoke
Smoke   Smoke   smoke

Smoke Smoke(resist)Smoke
Smoke   SmokeSmoke
Smoke Smoke Smoke
Smoke Smoke Smoke
Smoke Smoke Smoke
Smoke   SmokeSmoke
Smoke Smoke Smoke
Smoke Smoke Smoke
Smoke SMOKE SMOKE

XXII

♠ ♥ ♣ ♦

David is in the shower. Across the room, his Macbook pulses a small white light. Martin could walk over and open it right now. Martin could look through David's pictures. Martin could scan over the contents of David's folders. He could read David's old essays. He could find out whatever he wanted, probably. It is almost definitely a bad, bad idea to open David's Macbook. But he'd never have to know. How long does a shower take? A shower doesn't take that long. Maybe not now. Maybe another time. No, definitely not. Martin couldn't do something like that. He wouldn't.

The hotel walls seem to be very thin. Martin knocks out a hollow sound. He can clearly hear a conversation between a couple next door.

"Gerald? Gerald, I'm going to use your toothbrush, okay?"

"What? What, hold on. Say that again."

"I said I'm going to use your toothbrush."

"What, no. No – that's not okay. Don't use my toothbrush. Please don't tell me you were actually going to use my toothbrush."

"Are you serious? You're seriously refusing me access to your toothbrush?"

"Of course. Who shares a toothbrush? We are not a couple who share toothbrushes. You can do without a toothbrush for one night."

"Why should I? You're being ridiculous."

"I am being perfectly reasonable. It's just not on. Who does that? This is not cool, Sara."

"So you'll fuck me in my ass but you won't let me use your mouth stick."

"It's not like that. Don't phrase it like that. Just stop and think about it."

"Fuck you, Gerald. I can't deal with you when you're like this."

A door slams.

David emerges from the shower. His nipples make his chest look cross-eyed.

♠ ♥ ♣ ♦

Martin and David are taking a drive around Birmingham.

"I struggle to believe that there was ever a time when people re-used tissues," David says, "You know like those ones people stick in jacket pockets. What is up with that? It looks ridiculous."

"Did you know that a man's lifetime output of sperm, in relation to the number of eggs he fertilises, is roughly equivalent in ratio to the Earth's size in relation to our galaxy?"

"You just made that up," David says.

"Yeah. I did. Did it sound convincing? I've been rehearsing it for the last mile. I was waiting for you to say something so I could say that in response."

"Not really, sorry."

"Really? Why not?"

"I dunno. Numbers that large don't really mean anything to me. I don't really know how to deal with them," David seems a little depressed as he says this.

"What's the limit on what you can handle? What's the top number?"

"I dunno. An amount that something could cost maybe?"

"So what, like, a billion?"

"No. I don't know. How much does an island cost? How much does a skyscraper cost?"

"I don't know. How am I supposed to know that?"

Stairway to Heaven has come on the radio. Martin swings his lighter in a windscreen wiper motion. David looks very serious whilst Martin does this. With no encouragement, he desists. Each of Martin's actions require a degree of attention. Attention sustains Martin.

"So, why are we running away?"

"Because my dad is a dick."

"He doesn't seem like a dick. Your dad was always really nice to me."

"That's his thing though. He is nice to other people. He only takes it out on me."

"Seems like he'll forgive you for this, Martin."

"No – my dad is a dick. You want to know what kind of man my dad is? Once, I was on a train with him. We had to run for the train. We got on at the last minute, Coach M. My dad walked me all the way up the train's alphabet, through ten packed carriages, until we got to first class, to the two inches of extra legroom. When we got there, the carriage was almost empty. An old man was sat on his own in my dad's seat. My dad told the old man to move out of our seats."

For five minutes, a grey silence swells the car. There doesn't seem to be an appropriate point to end exploring, to pause an adventure.

"Do you think people with glasses find hugging awkward?" Martin asks, "I would be scared about my glasses falling off. That could be embarrassing."

"I dunno. Yeah, maybe."

"Are you annoyed with me or something?"

"No. Why would you ask that? Of course I'm not annoyed. Driving is just tiring I guess."

"Sorry. I shouldn't have asked."

"I know you don't want to drive after the incident, but I'm sure you can appreciate that it is tiring.

The phrase *He knows too much* booms in Martin's head. "Yeah, I get it. I do get it," he says.

"Sorry, I'll make more of an effort. Why don't we pull over for a smoke break? I need a smoke. I need a smoke really bad."

"How about I hold up a cigarette to your mouth so you can smoke and drive?"

"Is that legal? Seems like that shouldn't be legal."

"**Fuck** the system," Martin insists. "This will be good."

"Might be gay," David says. Martin has already started to light up two cigarettes. They splay off from each other like comedy fangs.

No turning back.

It feels generous.

It feels like an intimate gesture of trust.

It might well be gay.

It might be what love is.

David inhales deeply against Martin's fingers; far more deeply than a standard drag. Martin's fingers are a little damp. This is definitely gay. The radio is dead. Martin helps David to finish the cigarette in absolute silence.

XXIII

♠ ♥ ♣ ♦

Night falls. David is googling for clubs. It has been decided that a night of alcohol and women is a simple and effective way to reaffirm youth and masculinity.

"This is shit, Martin," David says, "Google doesn't have anything. This is the first time Google has failed me. Why don't people write reviews on clubs? It seems like something that should be reviewed."

"Maybe we could start a business reviewing clubs?"

"That sounds like a lot of work."

"Fun is hard work. Having fun is tiring."

"Fuck fun."

"Yeah, fuck fun."

♠ ♥ ♣ ♦

"IDs please, gentlemen," a bouncer demands.

Because of *the incident*, Martin only has a provisional driving licence. He feels emasculated presenting it to the bouncer, who is a foot taller and wider than him. The bouncer looks like a cheap waxwork. He has been inspecting Martin's ID for an unusually long time, looking back from the ID to Martin, from Martin to the ID.

"And how old are you, sir?"

Thoughtful pause.

"Twenty-one."

"Alright, get in."

The club is a part of the 'Vodka Revolution' chain corporation. Martin and David pay £4 to enter, and another pound to dump their coats. David has brought a bag.

"Bags are two," a stubby woman says.

"Two what?"

"Don't you get smart. Don't get smart with me. Bags are two quid." David hands her two pounds.

"Why did you bring a bag?" Martin asks, "I didn't realize you'd brought a bag."

"I don't know. I just picked it up when we left. I just did it, okay?"

From the entrance, Martin can see that the dance floor is empty, but the bar is four bodies deep. By the door, there is a short man wearing sunglasses and an inappropriately large coat. Below him is a black, shaggy dog, spread very flat over the club's sticky carpet. Its ears are folded down against the beating speakers. Martin catches the dog's eye. It looks miserable. The blind man is surrounded by three half dressed girls.

"Selfish bastard," David whispers into Martin's ear.

"The dog is a pulling tool. Maybe that guy is a genius," Martin shouts, transfixed by the dog's gaze.

"Selfish cunt," David whispers.

"The girls will never get with him. They just want to feel good about themselves."

"I like dogs."

"What, the girls?" They both laugh loudly, confirming their genius.

Martin barks at the dog a little, smiling. The dog doesn't seem to hear.

"I'll give you a tenner to kick the dog," David offers in a flat toned voice. Martin tries to pull a tempted expression.

"You're evil. I wasn't serious," David says.

Success

The club is filling. On the dance floor, people move in elaborately foreign postures. They jolt and jerk in ways that can only be explained by drugs. Hard core druggage is at work.

Martin and David move to the smoking area.

♠ ♥ ♣ ♦

Martin is speaking to a girl called Amy, who appears to be drifting in and out of consciousness. It is unclear if she is wearing a bra. It is cold out and Amy's nipples are saluting Martin.

"Hell is a smoking area where no one has a lighter."

"What?" Amy says.

"I said that hell is bad."

"Okay, yeah. What's your name again?"

"I'm Martin. I was saying before about who I am. Remember?"

Amy moves her head in what might be a nod.

"But it is complicated. I don't really know who I am. I mean, me on a gaming forum isn't me on Facebook," Martin explains to her chest. "I've got like ten different usernames now. That seems exhausting to say aloud. I haven't been one person in a long while. I like to make excuses, like, suggesting that no one is really one person. There's a comfort in universalising things like that, you know? You so rarely get caught out. I'm sure you could catch me out," Martin laughs a little to himself.

"*Igotta* find myfriends insidenow," Amy slurs out. Someone has left their mark in a thick green scrawl down her forearms. Martin can decipher the words, 'Suck' and 'Mum'. Her hair is dyed the colour of dehydrated pee.

"It seems like no one is perceptive. This club is structured like a Panopticon," Martin says, making a rare practical usage of his degree and immediately regretting it. "Not that it matters. You know, I've been so much more aware of this shit since I've been living online. When you're there, you're forced to present an exaggerated you." Martin makes an inverted commas gesture around the word 'you'. He regrets doing this also.

Something smells strongly of bile. It might be Amy. 'Anal' is written on her left bicep.

"When you spend too much time online, you can start to believe it, I think. I don't smell online. No one has bad hygiene on Facebook. Watching someone else view your Facebook is like an out-of-body experience."

The bile smell is definitely emanating from Amy. Her nipples seem more unsure now. One has faded. Her breasts are now winking at Martin.

"And that's not even the extent of it. I have a different me for different parts of my online life. Essentially, I feel like a dick all the time because I resent how people view me. I hate it so much. I resent that we're all complicit in doing this to each other."

Amy gags a little and slides a few inches

down

the

wall.

"You're wasting your time there, mate," David tells Martin over his shoulder.

"Life is a long, drawn out way of wasting time," Martin says as they return inside, leaving Amy to enjoy her evening.

The dance floor seems to be made up of couples. Two bodies appear to be a compulsory minimum. Martin notes the way that their lips pull apart and draw perfectly back together. They are like sexy magnets.

"Polarity," he thinks.

A thick baseline gropes at Martin's chest.

"I wonder what it would be like if we let a Polar Bear loose in the club," he says.

"What?" David asks.

"I said: 'I wonder what it would be like if we let a Polar Bear loose in this club,'"

"Yeah, me too."

♠ ♥ ♣ ♦

In the male toilets, CCTV cameras vie for a clear shot of Martin's penis. He feels wary of men who speak to each other while peeing. Excretion should never be a deep and profound experience.

Martin decides that all great philosophy is processed while shitting. The finest minds in western history must be united by their shared constipation.

Martin feels glad of David's company. His presence is comforting, like the smell of clean cotton.

♠ ♥ ♣ ♦

It is 2am and Martin's ears are throbbing. David shouts his initials across the club's cloakroom counter. Martin pictures his friend as a brash American: patronising locals in a foreign country with slow, stressed English.

"You should check it," he says, "Make sure that they've not stolen anything."

Inside, a white substance has lined David's bag. David picks at this crust a little, and then holds his finger under Martin's nose. It smells of mint. They simultaneously burst into laughter. Martin is laughing with a genuine glee. Martin feels good. He feels good for the first time in months. He smiles all the way back to their hotel.

XXIV

♠ ♥ ♣ ♦

"Cambridge next then," David announces the following morning.

"Wait, did we discuss that? I don't remember discussing that."

Their hangovers will settle in slowly. It is important to be careful right now. There is no need to argue.

"Really? I'm sure we discussed it. Maybe I dreamt it."

Martin faces away as David gets undressed. He feels innocent. He feels like a puppet. He feels no curiosity at all about the size and length and girth of David's penis.

"Cambridge is back _{south,} isn't it?" As a general rule, Martin resents going back on himself. On foot in particular, it feels like admitting defeat. Plus, he feels aware of everyone looking at him, like he is carrying an imposing backpack.

"Yeah. Whatever. That doesn't matter. Dude, you were totally like some Socrates type guy last night. Wandering around, challenging people's perceptions of things. It was deep."

"I'm a dick when I've been drinking," Martin says.

"That's not good, dude. You shouldn't admit that. People seem far too willing to admit what dicks they are." David is contorting his mouth like there's a hair caught somewhere on his tongue.

"I feel hateful. I'm in a mood to hate. Right now, I hate anyone different. A bigoted mood. Is that possible?"

"I guess it must be."

Martin's phone starts ringing. It is his mother. Who else would actually communicate via phone calls? His mother is probably the only person in the world to still use voicemail.

"Hi Mum."

David is plucking at his incisors.

"How's running away going, sweetie?"

"We're having fun, thanks Mum. How is everything? How is Dad?" Martin isn't interested in how things are, or how his Dad is. It's just what came out. The conversation seems surreal.

David has caught the hair. It dangles from his wetted thumb up against the winter daylight. It seems impossible that David's hair could be that long. He looks victorious and relieved.

"Everything is fine. Listen, my phone doesn't have a lot of battery, so I won't hold you up for long."

"Why call me when you have no battery? Did you assume that everything would be fine? What if I cut my leg open and was in Accident and Emergency?"

Spotting Martin's attention, David has fallen to his knees and is pumping his arms in mock-celebration, as though he has just scored an injury time goal in the World Cup final. Martin stretches his leg at full length in an attempt to kick at him, but just slips down the bed slightly.

"Don't be silly Martin. I know you can take care of yourself."

"I am going to spend all your money."

"You just be safe and tell us when you're coming home."

"I am going to spend all your money and I am going to go crazy."

"I have to go now, Martin. I love you."

The call terminates without her affection having been reciprocated.

"I think I've spent more time with The Simpsons than I have with my father," Martin says.

"D'oh," David says.

"Shut up."

"I want to lie in bed and be fed through a straw."

"D'oh," Martin says.

Martin has been on Wikipedia all afternoon, reading things he'd be better off not knowing.

He reads:

"The Ouroboros often represents self-reflexivity or cyclicality, especially in the sense of something constantly re-creating itself, the eternal return, and other things perceived as cycles that begin anew as soon as they end (the mythical phoenix has a similar symbolism). It can also represent the idea of primordial unity related to something existing in or persisting before any beginning with such force or qualities it cannot be extinguished."

Martin doesn't mind snakes. He likes the idea of a snake being bulimic. He remembers seeing a photograph of a snake that had eaten an alligator, and then burst. It had felt like a metaphor.

He writes a little poem to no one in particular:

How can I desire your affection,
now knowing that some infinities
are larger than others?

Martin can't remember the last time he had held a pen. He looks down at the poem and feels good. He has been productive today. Now he can have tomorrow off.

XXV

In Cambridge, Martin spits the length of his torso. The string of saliva swings against a subtle wind, pulling on his bottom lip before breaking like fruit from a bush. On the gum-pocked kerb, it lies like a long exclamation mark.

Martin and David are smoking outside Wetherspoons. *Brooding*. The air is heavy and full and cold and sharp; it is the tension between weathers.

Silences aren't nearly so notable online. The beauty of instant messaging is the artificial liberty to weigh and consider the composition of a phrase.

"I'm looking at these people, and I just can't process them. Why do they exist? Why are they living here? Why aren't they from London? If you insist on being from England, how can you not be from London? It's disgraceful. I don't get it, Martin. Martin? Martin, go ask them why they're not from London."

"You ask. Why would I ask that? Don't be dumb."

Inside the pub, a large and cheap looking wall-clock insists that it is 4.30. The drive took all day. Somehow, the pub is almost empty. Students are home for the Christmas break. There is a monotone atmosphere. The air fizzles like VHS. Martin and David are the pub's youngest patrons by a decade margin.

"Dude, let's compare scars! Scars always have good stories," David suggests.

"Yeah okay." Martin is wary of having sounded too keen and consciously slows down his next sentence. "I have scars all over my hands from cigarette burns and things."

"Nah, I mean good scars. Like, serious injury ones. Ones that you needed to go to hospital for," David is smiling as he says this. It is not a smile of sadism, it is a smile of excitement.

"I have lots of suicide scars," Martin says without apprehension.

David's face turns. "Oh, right. Yeah. I always forget." Unease and the first notes of beer blend in his voice.

"Yeah, it is probably easy to forget. Don't worry, man. It's cool. I never really talk about it. Not anymore. Not outside of therapy. The first time really was the biggest fuck up. The second time didn't do much. The airbag saved me. The first time, it wasn't even my bones, so much. They healed. The doctors said I have good bones. It was my teeth, they had to reset…"

David has interrupted. David is interrupting. David never interrupts. He is making *uh uhhhh* sounds. He is holding his palms out in a stop gesture. His eyes are closed.

"I don't really fancy playing any more, thanks," David is saying. "You've made it seem fucked now.

Seems perverse, sort of. I think I'd be better off not knowing about that stuff. That stuff about you. That's not the version of you I want to know, you know?"

"I understand," Martin says, swearing at himself internally. "Do you want another drink?" He stands, assuming David's response, and begins walking towards the bar. Martin feels ill. The bar seems very far away. The walk is practically a trek. It is almost a pilgrimage, like fetching water from a well.

Parched

Reset

Martin feels a strong sense of sympathy towards alcoholics in this moment.

The barman appears feminine, but addresses Martin in a low tone, as though he were speaking underground. Its name badge says 'Kenneth'.

"Two lagers, please." Kenneth nods; pulls the beers. "We are on our honeymoon," Martin says. He says this like a worn, hardened lie.

"Congratulations. Happy bumming."

Martin smiles, slightly ashamed. He slides money across to Kenneth and takes the beers. Was that as inappropriate as it sounded? Is Martin offended? He feels offended. As a straight man, he feels offended.

Perhaps Kenneth is not really an employee. Perhaps Kenneth is stealing from the tills. Perhaps Martin is on a reality show and David has set up this whole situation. Perhaps Ant and Dec are crouched under the bar, about to do some big, camp reveal.

Martin looks up, trying to spot a single, mischievous strand of confetti that might have managed to escape from the rafters.

David half-snatches his drink from Martin's hand and gulps desperately.

Quenched

"Hey, what do you think natural causes are? Like you know when people die of 'natural causes'. What does that constitute? Is it possible any more?" Martin rambles. "Like cancer is natural, but it doesn't count as a 'natural cause'. If a tree fell on you, would that be a natural cause? Trees are natural. Can a tree die of old age? Surely the only things that don't count as natural causes would be like, stabbings and shootings."

"I don't know. It's hard to imagine being old. You only die of natural causes if you're old. Like, I don't think I could die of natural causes yet. It's odd to think that's what old people aspire to. To die of 'natural causes'."

"It's weird to think that our generation aren't going to be lonely old people. It seems like a good thing to me, knowing that we'll always have the Internet."

"Money is comforting," David says into his beer.

A moment passes.

"*Fuck the budget,*" Martin says, "Let's buy something really big and pointless. Let's go crazy. Let's spend loads. Fuck my parents. Fuck money."

"Go crazy in Cambridge? Seems silly, man. We'll triple their economy."

"Is there a casino here?"

"I doubt it. It's Cambridge. What do they want with a casino?"

"I don't believe that people in Cambridge don't like to gamble. I would struggle to believe that."

"Okay then. What's the plan for going crazy?"

"Do you go crazy with a plan? Surely we shouldn't have a plan if we're going to go crazy?"

"We should probably get drunk then. Getting drunk seems like the obvious first step towards craziness."

Martin knows from experience that David is an awful drunk: very depressing and broody. The possibility of alternative drugs seems well out of reach.

"Let's go to a strip club first," Martin says. The plan rolls off his mind. He is an idea machine right now. Things are coming together. Everything's coming up Martin.

"Wait, are you serious? Can we do that? Can you just go to a strip club? Don't you have to like, book? Or be invited? I don't know how they work."

"My dad took clients to strip clubs. I think. It was only for a little while. He always had good stories about them. They sounded good when I overheard them. I think the most important thing is to have cash. I think strip clubs prefer cash. You can't swipe a card through breast trenches," Martin makes an exaggerated swiping action and licks his lips. There is a little hair on his top lip and his tongue tickles a bit.

David is smiling.

"Can you like, catch things in strip clubs? Like from sitting on the seats? I'm sure that's how you can get crabs. Wait, do we need to get changed? Surely we have to be in suits, like, looking important and significant."

"Yeah, maybe. Let's just see if we get in. If we don't, we'll do something else."

"Get in where? Do you know somewhere? Don't tell me you know a strip club in Cambridge. Dude, Martin: Cambridge is *not* the place to be going crazy. There's definitely no strip club in Cambridge."

"What, you think people don't have dicks in Cambridge?" Martin googles 'Strip Club Cambridge' on his phone. There are 847,000 results.

XXVI

♠ ♥ ♣ ♦

A taxi has dropped Martin and David outside of a strip club called *Sinners*. Between them, they have £600 in cash. The wad feels impressive in Martin's chest pocket. The wad is a second heart. Both Martin and David are quite tipsy. It will be a while before either of them is in need of another drink. It is likely that they will need to use the toilet rather soon. Before entering, they agree that when inside, they will speak as little as possible. They will move slowly and carefully.

"Shhh," David says, nudging his friend.

"IDs please gentlemen."

"Here you are, sir," Martin says with a flourish. The strip club bouncer does not take long to inspect. "As you can see, I am twenty-one."

"You going in then, fella?"

Sinners is open from 8pm. It is 8:30. There are around ten men in the club. The walls are lined with velvet. There's disco ball. There's a bar. There's a stage. Where's the toilet? There are tables and chairs facing the stage. There are menus on the tables. Where are the girls and where is the toilet?

Sinners runs by unarticulated rules.

Primal rules.

Grrrrr

There's an aura of prohibition.

The ten men are shadows. Unfulfilled, lonely shadows.

None are smiling.

Sad shadows.

Saddos

Two wear baseball caps.

Baseball caps are a sure sign that someone doesn't want to be disturbed.

Martin imagines fighting a man in a baseball cap. He imagines punching him so hard that steam comes out the man's ears and the baseball cap spins.

It seems that it is expected for the patrons to 'just know' what's cool and what's not.

Girls drift around the room. The girls appear to be women. The ten men do not speak to the girls. Speech seems dangerous.

The girls know what to do.

They are professionals.

Martin and David take seats up against the edge of the room.

It seems safest there.

Above them, a poster advert describes the club's girls as *RUTHLESSLY HOT*.

Drink deals are described as *FLAMING*.

Martin feels very aware that his trousers are touching the strip club's seat.

David motions for him to look across the room. A girl is grating her bottom into a man's jeans. The spectacle seems scary. Looking feels wrong.

Where's the toilet?

The man looks quite uncomfortable.

He smiles through his discomfort.

Etiquette on watching other people's dances seems unclear.

The dance looks like it should be making the girl's bottom very sore. Maybe her bottom is used to it. Her bottom is large. Maybe her bottom can handle the friction. Maybe it feels good. Maybe she is pretending to itch herself on him. Maybe this is a scratching club.

The girl – girl? – moves her body into an S-shape. Her scratching post turns away to sip at his bottle.

Martin wonders if someone will come up to him and cast him to be a porn star.

His porn star name is *All-in Alan*.

David's porn star name is *Floppy Turnriver*.

Martin isn't sure if he is happy. He isn't sure if he is enjoying this yet.

This is supposed to be crazy.

This is supposed to be an adventure.

Martin doesn't feel crazy. He feels a little sleepy and needs to pee. He can't leave David alone.

As Martin turns to ask David about peeing, a stripper approaches them.

"Want a dance?" she asks David.

"Ok*ay*," David says, his voice cracking a little.

David looks at Martin and gives him a curious thumbs-up. Martin returns the favour, without really knowing what it means.

The girl – girl? – has begun to bounce on David's lap. She is facing away from him. She places her hands on the back of her head. Her arms are very thin.

David isn't smiling. He is taking his dance very seriously.

Intense

Martin feels very aware that he is next. He is aware that in moments, a woman's buttocks will be working into his groin. He does not know how to mentally prepare for this. There seems to be a lot of pressure. His bladder feels full. His mouth feels dry. Martin can't imagine enjoying the dance under this much pressure. His hands are sweating.

Waiting is a complex torture. There's no virtue in patience. Not really. There is no value to a wait once it has ended.

Martin fucking hates waiting.

To Martin's right, a gruff man is watching porn on his iPhone. It is almost definitely porn. The man's lips look moist.

"Want a dance?" She comes out of nowhere. The stripper is chubby. She looks healthy. This girl looks more human than David's girl.

"Yes I do, please."

Politeness costs nothing.

Martin's palms are still very clammy. He doubts that his seat can take both their weights. Martin leans back into the wall as she climbs onto him. The girl definitely weighs more than he does.

Her dance begins slowly. It feels methodical. The girl faces him. There should be a rule against facing newbies.

"What's your name?" Martin says. The question slips out before he knows what has happened.

"Sparkle," she replies, grinding, looking over Martin's shoulder into the velvet wall

"Your name is Sparkle."

"My name is Sparkle," says Sparkle, pushing her bottom aggressively into Martin's crotch.

"Nice to meet you Sparkle."

"Aren't you charming?" Sparkle's voice is northern. Her hair is parted in two strict convulsions.

"I'm Martin."

"Martin Charming. Charming Martin. Here's a treat for you, Martin." Sparkle presses her breasts into Martin's face. Her bra is covered in sequins and it scratches a little. Martin thinks he caught a hint of nipple. His penis remains very much flaccid. He has no idea when the dance will end. It seems unclear how a stripper knows when to end a dance. Don't dances require music?

Martin thinks about waltzing with Sparkle at one of his parent's parties. She coughs a little.

"You are pretty."

"You got any blow?"

"Blow?"

"Yeah, blow."

"No. No blow."

"You want to get crazy, Charming Martin?"

"I am crazy. I'm a crazy guy. I am in a strip club."

"Getting crazy will cost you. You've got to pay to be crazy."

"I can afford to be more crazy."

David is on his second girl. David is a professional. He knows what he is doing. Martin makes a smiling, nodding movement to him.

"That's Glitter," David says, pointing to the human on his lap. Glitter's meagre breasts are pushed up and together. They look like tanned scoops of ice cream.

"Glitter and Sparkle."

"You want to get crazy with Glitter?" Sparkle says, "It will cost you."

"Sparkle and Glitter."

"That's right, baby."

"Why aren't you from London?"

"What?"

"Okay."

Sparkle gets off Martin's lap and sits next to him. The dance has ended more abruptly than Martin expected. He feels unsure whether to pay her now, or wait a while. He doesn't know what is a good amount to pay. There should be a pricing policy hung up somewhere.

"No blow?"

"No blow."

"Then how about you buy me a drink?"

"Okay."

Martin welcomes the chance to move away. He needs the toilet very badly. He can see the toilet behind the bar. The toilet is mocking him and his flaccid penis.

Martin pays £8 for a beer. The barman is wearing a leather waistcoat. He has a pierced eyebrow.

"There you go," he says, handing her the beer. His excursion didn't last nearly as long as he had hoped for. He wonders if he can run away to the toilet now.

"Beer? Okay then. You not joining me?"

"The beer was £8."

"Well, getting crazy's going to cost you," Sparkle repeats, scratching herself.

"We are professional bingo players," Martin says, "Have you ever played Bingo?"

"Bingo? That's for old ladies."

"We are also professional poker players. Do you play poker?"

"I can play that a bit, I guess. I know Texas Hold Them. I played with a client last year. I played strip poker at his birthday."

"Will you play with us? Can you come and play strip poker with us? That'd be pretty crazy, right?"

"That could be crazy. Okay. I get off at midnight."

"David," Martin says, beckoning. "This lady is going to play Strip Poker with us."

"I'm down with that," Glitter says, interrupting. She smiles broadly at Sparkle and nods. Her teeth look jaundiced.

"Okay, sure," David says. David looks serious, as though he is trying hard to be cool. "Glitter is taking me to get a tattoo," he adds.

"What? Really? You're getting a tattoo? Just like that?"

"Glitter knows a guy. He'll give us a good deal."

"You don't even know what a good deal on a tattoo is," hisses Martin suspiciously.

"I'm getting the Ace of Spades."

"You mean the PokerStars logo."

"No, not the PokerStars logo. The Ace of Spades."

"The Ace of Spades is the PokerStars logo, David."

"Look, you're welcome to come. Maybe you should get one too, if you're so crazy."

"I'm crazy all right. I could get a tattoo if I wanted a tattoo."

Martin feels very stressed. Strip clubs are not relaxing at all. There should have been some kind of educational tape in school to warn against strip clubs.

"I need to pee," he tells the group.

"I will come with you," David suggests. "Stay right here, girls."

Martin moves quickly away. David has to catch up.

"What the fuck are we doing," Martin says, "I don't want to fucking play fucking strip fucking poker. Maybe there are windows in the toilets. Maybe we can escape."

"Dude, why would you want to escape? This is great. I really do need to pee though. Come on."

David pulls Martin through the Gents door, leading with his shoulder. Both of them are careful not to touch it. Martin wonders if there is any need for a Ladies toilet at a strip club.

2009

♠ ♥ ♣ ♦

Martin is throwing a single dart at the board on his dorm room door. He has been trying to hit triple-twenty for two hours. He is pacing back and forward like someone with a legitimate problem. He feels determined. He is being stubborn. He is being very, very stubborn.

Persistence

Martin has two essays due in under twenty-four hours time. He has started neither. At this moment in time, triple-twenty remains the absolute priority.

In two hours, Martin has a meeting with his supervisor to discuss his dissertation progress.

This morning, Martin took a pretty awful beat in a $33 six max sit 'n' go on Full Tilt. 5♠6♠ on the button, he raises half pot and gets one caller. Flop comes 478 rainbow. Martin has the absolute nuts. He checks, and his caller shoves. Martin insta-snaps and sees his rival holding 7♠6♥. Turn 7♣. River 6♦.

Martin barely managed to restrain himself from putting a fist through his laptop screen.

This is not a good mood for discussing progress. This is a mood for dart throwing.

One time

♠ ♥ ♣ ♦

Martin's supervisor has published three books: two on the Philosophy of Science and the other on Alfred North Whitehead. Her office is windowless and lined with hardback books. Her office is essentially a closet.

A miniature fan looks back and forth between the room's occupants. It churns the closet's sour air. It is making an inordinate amount of noise. The fan is the room's centerpiece. Everything exists in relation to the fan.

"Is there anything you need to tell me, Martin?"

"No."

"Are you enjoying this term so far?"

"It's okay. It's fine."

"And how are you getting on with your seminar group?"

"They're okay. Everything's fine."

"It's okay to speak with me Martin. I do care, despite what you think."

"Thanks. I'm fine."

"Are you pleased with your essays?"

"They're okay."

"I see."

Martin scans the shelves. He likes books with pictures.

"Do any of these books have pictures?" he asks.

"No, I don't believe they do."

"Thank you for your time."

XXVII

♠ ♥ ♣ ♦

A man named Kevin owns the tattoo parlor. The parlor is called *INKLINGS*. *INKLINGS* is in the basement of a Nail Salon. Glitter and Sparkle seem familiar with Kevin. They greet him with hugs. Martin thinks that the hugs must clearly indicate that Kevin has been inside of both of them on multiple occasions.

Kevin's tattoos start at the top of his neck and don't stop. A long ponytail hangs down his back, greasier by each inch. The ponytail looks vulnerable. Martin represses the desire to yank on Kevin's ponytail. Kevin's neck is as large as Martin's thigh. Martin's hands wouldn't be able to handle its girth.

Girth

Kevin's Adam's Apple looks like a tumor. It is a tumor in an elevator.

"Who are these guys?" Kevin asks, facing away from Martin and David.

Martin represses a desire to reach for David's hand.

"This here is Charming Martin and his pal David. They're looking to get some tattoos," Glitter says, twirling a finger through her hair.

Kevin looks Martin and David up and down. Martin feels naked, stripped by Kevin's gaze. He has said nothing about wanting a tattoo. Everything has been assumed. All bad things seem to begin from assumption.

"They got cash?"

"We've got cash," David says.

Kevin's eyes narrow, spying his prey. It is apparent that David was not being addressed.

"So you girls have brought me some cash cows tonight? Very nice job, ladies. It's always nice to have some pretty company and lucrative business." Martin feels naked and cold and small. "Which of you boys is first?" Kevin says.

Martin nudges David forwards.

"I am, I guess," David says, stammering.

"You guess? You can't be guessing about a tattoo, son. This is the real deal. This isn't some wash off shit."

"Okay," David says, "I know. Man. Sir."

"Do you know what you want?"

"I want the Ace of Spades, please."

"Please sir, the Ace of Spades sir!" Kevin says, laughing. "I'm just shitting you kid. That's a good choice. A fine choice. A great first tattoo."

David begins unbuttoning his shirt.

"Whoa there son, slow down. Hell, I wish the girls were as fast to get their clothes off. I have to do your design first."

"Oh right," David says. Martin can tell that he seems unsure whether or not to button his shirt back up.

"Let's go for a smoke while the design gets done," Martin says.

"You go for it boys." Kevin's permission sounds like nectar.

"This will be our last chance to run," Martin says once they are outside, "You will remember me telling you that this is our last chance and be like 'Oh, Martin! Why didn't I listen to you. I am dumb and stupid.' You'll wish that we ran right now. Besides, dude, our strippers have really pointy elbows."

"I am getting a tattoo and so are you," David says, "When else in your life are you going to hang out with strippers? Come on man, we're supposed to be going crazy. This is an adventure, right?"

Martin feels like he wants to rip up something very dense and sturdy. He wants to smash something valuable. He wants to scratch at something very malleable.

"**ARGGGGH**," he screams.

"*Martin, what the fuck?*" David whispers, as if to counter balance Martin's noise level.

"I don't know, David. I don't know *Idon'tknowIdunno* I don't know I don't knooooooowI.Don'T.Know.I don't know."

Martin masks his face with laced fingers. His hands smell of cigarettes and flesh. He feels corrupt. He feels immoral. He feels like shit. He doesn't know what is going on or what to do and it all seems fucked and...

"Look, mate. You don't have to get a tattoo. Just sit in with me while I get one."

"No. If we are going to do this, *we may as well do it right.*" Martin sighs, throwing his butt into the kerb. "Didn't I say that it was too late to get a band's logo tattooed on me? Well maybe it's not. Maybe I want that now."

"I'm proud of you," David says.

"I'm proud of me too."

"What you going to get?"

"I'm going to get a band logo, of course."

"Nice, Martin. What band?"

"It doesn't matter. I don't know. The Who maybe? I think that I could pull off a little RAF ring. It'd look patriotic, maybe."

"Yeah. Kick ass, man."

Martin looks to the sky. He looks, hoping that it might mean something. Without a cigarette in his hand, Martin has become acutely aware of the wind and the cold, the winter's sharpness. In the near distance, the crest of a storm hangs over some Gothic spires. Martin's neck has started to hurt.

"Let's get back inside. It's fucking freezing." Down steps, in the parlor, on the chair, a commitment awaits him. A tattoo: an unplanned commitment. Martin considers that this is what pregnancy must feel like.

"You boys ready?"

Kevin is sat to the side of a leather chair, postured like a dentist. Martin considers the possibility that he might have to pay for yearly check ups on his tattoo, yet another thing for his schedule – his busy, busy schedule.

David retakes his seat in the leather recliner.

"Open wide," Martin says as David unbuttons his shirt for the second time. Glitter and Sparkle pretend to swoon. Kevin gently applies a wet piece of paper to David's chest and carefully peels off the outline of a spade.

"So this is really happening," David says.

The needle starts to whirr.

XXVIII

♠ ♥ ♣ ♦

Kevin instructed Martin and David to keep the cling film on for three hours. They must wash their new scars with soapy water and apply the special skin cream that Kevin sold them three times a day.

The combined procedures cost in excess of £250, a price worthy of craziness. On his arm, Martin bears a larger-than-anticipated red, white and blue circle.

It's the wrong way round

Martin is yet to pay any money to the strippers. The prospect of paying them seems daunting.

Martin's tipsiness is long gone. Somehow, David's original plan has remained intact. It has worked out precisely: Glitter and Sparkle have accompanied the boys back to their hotel. Each couple enters separately. Martin and Sparkle. David and Glitter. Discreetness seemed like a simple courtesy. The receptionist had not looked up. Martin feels like he could be a philandering footballer.

Phil-and-durrrr

The hotel maids will come into their room tomorrow morning and see their detritus, the evidence of their debauchery. They will wonder how best to sell their story to The Sun.

Polygamy

The strippers don't seem mysterious any more. At this point, the prospect of seeing them naked seems to be a little ridiculous. Martin feels amicable towards Glitter and Sparkle. They have been through trauma together. They are friends. Martin's arm feels sore. Sparkle had held his hand through the tattooing. He did not sob. During the procedure, Martin had internally occupied himself with mourning his innocence.

David is counting out four rows of chips. Stacks will begin at ten thousand, with the big blind at one hundred, increasing every eight minutes. Rules have been established. The group will play standard no-limit Hold 'Em. Upon each show down, the individual holding the losing hand will be required to remove one item of clothing. Losing an all-in requires instant nudity. Martin and David are taking a socks and jacket handicap.

Martin is sat on the floor feeling good. He feels sore, but good. David winces each time Glitter sways into his newly branded chest. Glitter's bare torso is corrugated by fine stretch marks. Seeing David wince makes Martin feel less alone.

After just five hands, Martin has taken a strong chip lead. His J♠K♥ out-flopped David's Queens. Getting David to remove his clothes felt slightly gay and pointless. However, Martin feels confident and giddy.

Everyone seems to be having a great time. Everyone is happy.

Happiness

Glitter has excused herself to pee three times. Martin is 80% sure that she is leaving to do drugs in the bathroom. Glitter's habit is slowing down the play. She has no respect for blinds. Martin sort of feels annoyed that he hasn't been offered some drugs. What if he had wanted some drugs? He could handle drugs. Martin reckons that he can list around ten different drugs.

"Mate, it's on you."

Martin looks down to 8♥8♣. Snowmen in the hole. *Life is good again.*

"Raise to five hundred."

"I'm all in I guess," Glitter says.

"What, really?"

"You scared Charming Martin? It's eight-thousand more for you." Glitter laughs to Sparkle.

"No. I guess not. I guess I call."

"Two Aces," she says, "That's good right?" She laughs, loudly, viciously. There is a thumping from the far wall, a muffled cry of *KEEP IT DOWN*.

Martin's penis is indeed very flaccid. Very down.

David avoids Martin's eye. He stares at the Eights. Martin knows that the call was terrible. He knows that he will be punished. Of course, he has to be punished.

David deals out a board of 5♠5♣6♠J♦Q♦.

Punishment

Martin loses his trousers. Both girls still have every important bit covered.

The room is slightly chilly.

It is 2am.

2009

♠ ♥ ♣ ♦

Martin's latest therapist likes to be called John. This is their third weekly meeting. John has a crucifix above his door. Martin knows that John used to be a Catholic priest. This seems comforting.

John's office resembles the conservatory of a fancy hotel. Despite being on the sixteenth floor, bathed in an abundance of daylight, John has various artificial light sources scattered about the room. The most notable of these is John's imposingly professional looking desk lamp, which is generating a stifling mixture of heat and luminescence onto Martin's periphery vision.

Martin feels willing to learn. He feels willing to be therapised. As John speaks, he is toying with the rather cool idea that to an outside spectator, he might seem to be under police interrogation in some low budget film-noir.

John is training Martin in a psychological discipline called cognitive-behavioural-therapy. So far they have worked over Martin's uses of humour as a defence mechanism, his insecurities about religion and his general resentment towards women. John says that Martin needs to re-train the way he thinks about these things, the way he approaches his own thoughts.

Martin feels progressive. He feels healthy. He feels willing to learn.

"What do you mean, 'grow up'?" Martin says.

"You know what I mean, Martin."

"No – I really don't. Give me some clear boundaries."

"Growing up is having self discipline. It is taking care of your physical and mental health. It is independence."

"But I did that at university."

"Did you? Didn't you say last time that university was just a good way to delay becoming a 'real human'?"

"That sounds like something I would say."

"So what is it to be a human, Martin? A real human?"

"I guess you need to have faith in stuff. Faith in money."

"Then have faith!"

"But I don't have any faith left, John. I feel as though I can't trust anything. Nothing seems real. I reckon that if I were to have some grounding point; some stability to build upon, then I could actually try to be sure of something."

"You're chatting shit," John says. This seems refreshing. Martin knows that John is right, but he isn't sure what he's right about.

"You put your faith in different things every day. You might not always call it faith, but that's what it is. You put faith in your bus driver, a stranger with your life in his hands. You've got to have faith to cross the road, blindly hoping that each sitting car won't accelerate at you. And everyone has to put their faith in money. Money runs on a system of faith, otherwise, it doesn't really mean anything. It's just a representation of something."

In his degree, Martin had learned that money is a 'transferrable, exchangeable storage of labour'. You have to believe that the person on the other end of each transaction will uphold their part of the contract.

"However: when people put all their faith in money," John says, "They will begin to worship it. They lose sight of the fact that money means nothing. Then they wonder why money hasn't made them happy! Money doesn't make people happy, because it's just blind faith with no objective reality behind it. Money has no context. People tend towards worshiping something, Martin, because they want the kind of stability that you have described. You have learnt how easily faith in money can collapse. That's a lesson worth paying for. Now, you need to discover what is really worth worshipping."

"What are you saying?"

"I'm saying that reality isn't conspiring against you. I'm saying that you have to be willing to learn."

Willing
to
learn

Willing
to

learn

Leaning
to
Worm
(heehehehehehehheeheheheheh)

♠ ♥ ♣ ♦

XXIX

The M11 looks bleak: bleak and cold and wet. Martin is drawing a swastika in the passenger side window's condensation. Nothing seems inappropriate any more.

Watching the motorway, Martin's focus shifts to the window itself. He picks one raindrop to be the hero. Like all heroes, he begins alone, but soon, the raindrop swings right against the wind and swells with allies. The drop is forcing its way through veiny defences, all varicose with danger for this young warrior. By the window's base, the drop is an army – now melting, worn from battle, giving itself over to a rubber sealant grave. His quest will be celebrated for generations. He shall not be forgotten.

♠ ♥ ♣ ♦

The decision not to call the police was mutual. It seemed far, far too embarrassing. Impossibly, terrifyingly embarrassing. To call the police would be to admit failure, to concede. If they called the police, they would have to admit that they had been mugged by strippers. Martin would have had to give his phone number, his home address.

Defeat

After Martin stacked off with eights, the strippers didn't look back. Within twenty minutes, the strippers had felted both of them. Looking glum and feeling worse, Martin and David went out onto their hotel balcony for a cigarette. They stood in their pants, conspiring. They hoped that the fresh air would rally them, sober them up. When they returned, they would up the stakes; regain their money and their pride. It would be the comeback of a lifetime.

The strippers told them to shut the door – that it was cold; that they'd set off the fire alarm. A moment after Martin complied, Glitter ran over and turned the lock, sealing them on the balcony. They could only watch as the strippers went through their wallets.

Somehow, David's car keys and laptop had remained. The keys, the laptop and the tattoos.

At least they had the tattoos.

The Mod stamp remains.

The Mod stamp is tingly, sore evidence.

The tattoos were proof of an adventure.

On the balcony, Martin had repressed the desire to tell David that it was his fault, that Glitter was his girl. It was mid-morning before the cleaner saved them. Once inside, Martin had to repress the desire to post a lengthy and detailed Facebook post, explaining the situation.

No one can ever know

David glares out at the endless motorway.

"You know, we never saw them naked," Martin says. "They stripped us. Financially and emotionally, we were stripped by strippers." As Martin begins laughing, David turns up the radio.

There will be no sing along.

"Hey, why do we only use inches for Pizzas, Subways and knobs?"

They are returning home.

2010

♠ ♥ ♣ ♦

Martin is watching videos of Phil Ivey on YouTube.

Phil Ivey is widely regarded as the best all-round living poker player, and many professionals argue that he should be regarded as the best of all time. Last year, Ivey made the final table of the World Series of Poker Main Event, a statistically phenomenal achievement. Despite going into the final table holding only around 5% of the chips in play, Ivey was listed at 6/8 to take the title. In the end, he was eliminated in seventh place after his Ace King couldn't hold against Ace Queen all in pre-flop. He was the only player at that Final Table with any World Series of Poker bracelets, which are awarded for winning a World Series tournament. In fact, Ivey has eight bracelets, the joint-fifth most of any player in the history of the Series. Despite his fame coming almost exclusively off the back of his expertise in Hold 'Em, all eight of Ivey's bracelets have come from victories in non-Hold 'Em tournaments.

Called 'The Tiger Woods of Poker', Ivey is tall, good-looking and impossibly rich. Ivey finds his way into hundreds of poker articles each year. He is the headline of any tournament that he plays. His life is just a Google search away. There, you can trace his biography, his career, his achievements, his earnings. Like Martin, you can even watch him play.

What you won't be able to do is imitate him.

Ivey does not play the manic aggressive style of his younger peers. Neither does he play the tight, conservative style of the more veteran generation. Ivey plays a style entirely of his own. Ivey seems to treat each hand as an individual moment, dismissing all the robotic complacency that many online professionals depend on.

Ivey appears to be in control at every stage in a hand, even when check calling out of position. Ivey has a plan, but Ivey can adjust. Ivey's plan is to get all your chips. Ivey is ruthless. Ivey makes the most impossibly difficult decisions, and makes them correctly. What happens after that is just in the cards.

Martin is watching a cash game hand played between Ivey and Jason Mercier, a young tournament expert. The title of the video is 'Most Well Played TV Poker Hand I've Seen'. The clip is from a show called High Stakes Poker. In High Stakes Poker, a specific number of hands are played in each session. The hand in the video is towards the very end of the session.

Gus Hansen opens the action with a raise to $4,200, holding Q♣6♦. Eli Elezra calls with 9♣5♣. From the button, Ivey flats with 9♠9♦. In the small blind, Jason Mercier three bets with A♥4♥ to $22,100. Gus and Eli fold, and Ivey calls in position, smiling, distracted by a conversation at the other end of the table. Jason remains stone faced and silent.

The flop comes 2♠3♦7♥, giving Jason a gutshot, an overcard, and the back-door nut flush draw. Ivey has flopped an overpair. Jason swiftly leads with a continuation bet of $28,700 – around half the pot. There is no chance that Ivey folds in this spot. He has turned serious. He riffles chips, pouts and counts out a raise to $78,700, representing the exact hand he has – two nines can't comfortably see many turn cards. At this point, Ivey is hoping to take down the pot. The commentator, Gabe Kaplan, assumes that the hand is over, but Jason sits, riffling chips in both hands. After a minute, he announces "I'm all in." At this point, Ivey's eyes flash up. Jason is all in for $185,100. By this move, Jason is selling a very convincing story. His line is strong. He is representing either a pair that beats Ivey's, or a flopped set. To call, Ivey would need $107,000. He would be getting around 3:1 on his money, so Ivey only needs to be good around one-in-three times for this to be a mathematically sound call, however, with Jason's incredibly convincing line, it seems impossible that this could be one of those times. Jason's bet has a large amount of fold equity.

At this point, the rest of the table has gone quiet. They know that they are watching genius at work. Ivey is visibly torn. At this point, he does not need to supress his emotions. He glances at Mercier.

"Alright," he says, kissing his teeth. "Guess you got me here. If you got the overpair, you got me." He holds a stack of chips under Mercier's nose and drops them into the pot.

Jason remains professional, unfazed, and asks, "Once or twice. I have Ace high."

"Two nines," Ivey says. The rest of the table is standing. The pot is worth $425,200.

"Twice, or once?" Mercier asks.

"I only wanna do it once," Ivey says, his fist against his jaw.

The camera cuts to Phil Laak pulling his hoodie around his face. The table is in shock. Jason has seven outs and 32% equity. His hand will win around one-in-three times in this spot.

"I suddenly feel not-so-bad about putting the two-hundred thousand with my two Queens," Gus Hansen says, drawing a big smile from Ivey.

The turn comes the 8♣. Jason dejectedly throws his chips to the middle of the table and sighs a big "Aww, man." Ivey stares at the board.

The river comes the Q♠.

"Nice hand," Jason says.

"Welcome to the Ivey world, Jason," Eli Elezra says.

Martin is in rapture. Ivey is a mystical experience.

XXX

♠ ♥ ♣ ♦

"Let's just agree that if you want to be yourself, you can be yourself in private." Martin's father is in a dressing gown. It is hard to seem stern in a dressing gown.

"So you forgive me then?"

"For what? Being a fuck up? I can excuse you for that. Fuck ups are everywhere. It'd be ludicrous of me to expect anything more from you. I was a fuck up for a long time. I'm still a bit of a fuck up now. You think I value my work? You think I care about what I do? I do it to provide, Martin. Look, I don't hate you: I just want you out of my way, son."

"I'm a connoisseur of awful people," Martin says.

"You don't impress me, Martin. Don't you try to impress me with that shit. Just tell me what you want."

"I want the old house," Martin says.

"*Done*. Have it. Whatever. Go."

Martin gets out of his father's way, up the stairs and into his room. The windows are cracked open. The air is fresh. Everything remains.

There is the stain. There is Martin: a stain on the house, a stain on the world. There is Martin's life work: hidden under the desk; kept secret, kept safe.

As soon as Martin logs on to his computer, it is as though nothing has happened. The reassuring familiarity of his profile remains. Remains regardless. Remains spitefully, mockingly.

Eighteen notifications and thirty-five emails sit patiently, waiting for his attention. Facebook informs Martin that his personal trainer and a girl from his university halls share this birthday. This detail seems okay – acceptable.

Suddenly

a revelation _{falls} upon him.

It shimmers down the ridge of his nose, like a dancing itch.

Martin rubs at his nose like a Genie's lamp.

The idea begins to form.

Martin has to delete his Facebook.

The moment feels seminal. Martin feels profound as he rattles the Facebook account section, looking for a delete function. Sparks of catharsis feed his fingers.

People have roles in social groups. Martin's role is to teach his friends how to snipe on eBay and to remove spiders from rooms without harming them (and thus incurring their wrath).

Martin will be deleting his presence from 731 friends. He will be removing himself from 423 photographs, two videos and six notes. Martin is going to escape from the digital freezer of all experience, sensation and memory.

Liberation

A panicked clicking ensues. The function is hiding from him. This is Facebook resisting, fighting back. It doesn't want to let Martin go. Remember the good times we had together, Martin. All those hours together, do they count for nothing?

This is social suicide. This is the third suicide attempt.

This one won't fail.

Eighty-two friends on chat.

A high-score on Snake.

Twenty-three unread messages.

Delete Account

Submit

You are about to permanently delete your account.

Are you sure?

Epilogue, 15 April 2011

♠ ♥ ♣ ♦

Martin knows there was never a time when everything was great in the world; that the past only seems special and fun because of how memories and history are represented. He knows that reality has always sucked, and that life has always been hard. He admits that his generation is probably no more fucked than any other.

Some day, Martin's generation will run the world. Some day. But not today.

Martin opens up Full Tilt Poker. The program doesn't seem to be working.

"Is Full Tilt working for you?" Martin asks David on Gmail chat.

"Hang on, let me check. You try their website."

On Full Tilt Poker's website, there is a notice from the FBI: *This domain name has been seized by the U.S. Immigrations and Customs Enforcement – Homeland Security Investigations, Office of the Special Agent in Charge, Baltimore, Md. in accordance with a warrant obtained with the assistance of the U.S. Attorney's Office for the District of Maryland, and issued pursuant to 18 U.S.C. § 981 and 1955(d) by the U.S. District Court from the*

District of Maryland. It is unlawful to conduct an illegal gambling business in violation of 18 U.S.C. § 1955 and property used in violation of that section is subject to seizure and forfeiture pursuant to 18 U.S.C. § 1955(d).

"No, it's not working for me either."

"Looks like it is fucked. Looks like the domain has been seized by the FBI."

"Oh shit. Maybe they've actually got Durrrr hostage."

Martin loads up PokerStars. It too is down. Their website bears the same message.

"Stars is down too."

"Dude, have you seen 2p2? People are going mad," David says. "Seems fucked."

"I just had the best run of sneezes," Martin says.

"That's sweet. I love that stuff. When I woke up, I spent twenty minutes just looking at my dick. I wasn't playing with it or anything; I was just giving it a thorough inspection," David says.

"That sounds good too."

Acknowledgments

♠ ♥ ♣ ♦

Thank you to James Tadd Adcox, DJ Berndt, Richard Chiem, Frances Dinger and Frank Hinton for helping me to develop as a writer.

Thank you to my friends and editors Michael Seidlinger and Kyle Muntz. Thank you for believing in nineteen year olds.

Thank you to my family.

Thank you to all my housemates.

Thank you to the University of York Poker Society.

Thank you to Isabel Rogers for saving my life.

Thank you to all the writers whose words and thoughts are reformed here.